PRAISE FOR MIA
AND HER BOOKS

"Mia Hopkins knows how to put characters on a page."
—*Heroes and Heartbreakers*

"Beautifully descriptive...hot, sexy and full of yearning!"
—Delilah Devlin, bestselling author

"Mia Hopkins is an imaginative author who doesn't take the easy road to a formulaic book."
—*USA TODAY*

"Off the charts hot."
—*The Romance Studio*

"And those sex scenes...Holy hotness!"
—*Crystal Blogs Books*

"Sweet and filthy at the same time, just the way I like it. This book made me so happy."
—*Read All the Romance*

"I absolutely adored every inch of this book."
—*The Romance Reviews, Top Pick*

COWBOY PLAYER

A COWBOY COCKTAIL BOOK

Mia Hopkins

Little Stone Press
LOS ANGELES

Edited by Jennifer Haymore
Cover by Syneca

Cowboy Player/ Mia Hopkins. -- 1st ed.
ISBN-10:
0-9979922-9-8
ISBN-13:
978-0-9979922-9-8

To Valerie and Sharilynne. My beautiful virgins.

To Jennifer Miller, for continuing to laugh at my corny jokes.

To Michelle. I'm so lucky to have a sister like you. Thank you for sacrificing your best adolescent years to babysit me.

To my husband, Brent, whose eyes are sage green rimmed with blue. I love you.

And most of all...to every girl who's been knocked down by love but keeps getting back up. You indestructible badass. This one's for you.

CHAPTER ONE

The Peach

*I wonder how many people I've looked at all my life
and never seen.*

—JOHN STEINBECK

Eight o'clock in the morning. A giant yawn cracked Melody Santos's jaw as she took two vacuum-sealed rib-eye steaks out of the van and shut the door. She glanced at her reflection in the back window. Bags under her eyes, no makeup. With a sigh, she tucked a few loose strands of hair behind her ear, pulled up the zipper on her hoodie and went back to work.

MacKinnon Ranch was a two-hour drive from Santa Monica, home of one of the biggest farmers' markets in Los Angeles County. For the past year, her friend Clark MacKinnon had been selling his family's grass-fed beef at similar markets all over the state. Always on the prowl for odd jobs, Melody had been giving him a hand for the past two weeks, ever since the school year ended. The work wasn't difficult, but the hours on the road could be brutal.

After Melody bagged up the steaks and thanked the customer, she stifled a second yawn. Clark glanced at her out of the corner of his eye and smiled. He shoved his big hands into the pockets of his Carhartt jacket. "Hang in there, Santos."

A young woman approached the booth. Her clingy exercise clothes showed off a tanned, toned body. A rolled-up yoga mat in a sling hung over her shoulder like a quiver without arrows.

"Hey there," she said to Clark in a sexy, scratchy voice. "Nice to see you again."

Clark turned to the woman. "Hey there, yourself. How's it going?"

Melody stepped back to give the cowboy and the yoga goddess some privacy. Lucky entered the booth, handed her a paper cup of coffee, and rolled his eyes. "Look at him. Chick magnet," he said under his breath.

Melody took a sip. "I think it's the cowboy hat."

"Hey, I wear a cowboy hat too. No one's jumping on my rig."

She covered her smile. Melody had known Lucero "Lucky" Garcia since he was a freshman recently immigrated from Mexico and she was the senior assigned to be his English tutor. Now twenty-four, Lucky worked as a ranch hand for the MacKinnons and competed as an amateur tie-down roper at rodeos. He was handsome but not as handsome as Clark, whose dark hair and classic good looks made him an easy mark for lovesick country and city girls alike.

As Melody drank her coffee, the sun broke through the clouds overhead. The beach was less than a mile away, and an ocean breeze stirred the yoga goddess's golden hair. With a smile, the woman whipped out her phone and handed it to Clark, who dialed in some numbers before handing the phone back.

Lucky and Melody watched the yoga goddess's perfect ass sashay away.

"What the hell is your secret?" Lucky asked. "How do I get me some ladies like that?"

Clark flashed his easy smile. "Ain't no secret."

"Tips. I need professional tips," said Lucky.

Melody had known Clark even longer than she'd known Lucky. The same age, they'd been close friends since they were old enough to walk. Clark had always been a joker and an insufferable flirt. She'd moved away after high school, but now that she was back in her hometown, they'd picked up their friendship exactly where they'd left off.

"Yeah, Clark," she teased. "Give us some tips on how to be a lady-killer."

"Tips, huh?" He turned to Lucky. "All right. Two tips. When you meet a woman, just look in her eyes and make a mental note of what color they are."

Melody snorted. "But what if her eyes are boring brown, like mine?"

"Your eyes aren't 'boring brown', Mel." Clark took his coffee from the paper tray resting on one of the coolers.

"Really? Then what color are they?" She covered her eyes with her hands.

Clark's voice came through the darkness. "They're coffee-colored. Dark roast. And there's a tiny streak in the iris of your left eye. On the bottom half. Shaped like a backwards Z. It's the color of a penny."

She laughed. "Stop making things up."

"I ain't making anything up."

Lucky gently pulled her hands down. "Lemme see." He leaned forward and searched her eyes up close, making her feel self-conscious.

"God, you two are so full of it," she said softly.

"No, Mel, he's right," Lucky said. "Look at that. Exactly right."

"Of course I'm right." Clark drank his coffee and gave her a self-satisfied grin.

"The eye thing, check," said Lucky. "What's step two?

"Step two's easy. Just let 'em talk. Then ask lots of questions."

"Are you serious?" Lucky said. "That's secret number two?"

Clark nodded. "That's it."

Melody leaned toward Clark. "So what did you ask the yoga goddess?"

Clark shrugged and said nothing.

She raised an eyebrow at him. "Ugh. You player. You know, we ladies are not as simple as that. Your pickup tricks wouldn't work on me."

"I'm going to go with Mel on this," said Lucky. "Looking in a woman's eyes and listening? That seems too easy."

"Trust me. Just try it."

"I will, Superman. First chance I get." Lucky rubbed his hands together in the cold morning air. Superman was Clark's childhood nickname. He hated it.

"So," said Melody, "what if *I* want to pick up a hot date? Do you think your strategies will work for me too?"

Clark looked her up and down as if assessing her. He was joking, but his scrutiny made Melody's cheeks unexpectedly warm. Clark nodded slowly to himself. "You've already got a lot of things going for you, Mel. You don't need my help. But if you feel like having some fun, I think I see my friend Jerome walking up the street."

Melody blinked, breaking eye contact with Clark and shaking off the uneasy feeling in her chest. What was wrong with her today? Maybe she was getting sick. "Who's Jerome?"

"He owns Le Monarque and a whole bunch of other restaurants in L.A. Good guy. I've been working on getting a contract with him for months." Clark's eyes twinkled. Melody knew that look. It meant trouble. "Tell you what. I'm going to pretend to be on the phone next to the van," he said. "You handle him and do what I said."

"Handle him? What are you talking about?" Melody asked. Lucky had already started to laugh.

"One, look into his eyes. Two, listen to him and ask questions." Clark took out his phone. "Weren't you paying attention to me?"

"What?" Melody put down her coffee cup. "No! Jesus, Clark, you're crazy. I'm not doing it."

Clark stood in front of the van and pressed his phone to his ear. "Go on, girl. Shake it. Lucky, go count tri-tips in the van. This is Mel's show."

Lucky disappeared. Melody had just enough time to wipe the anger off her face before a tall, tattooed man in a black T-shirt, black jeans and black motorcycle boots approached the booth. An entourage of beleaguered-looking cooks in chef's whites followed him, pushing a cart stacked with crates of produce. The man in black had longish black hair and a boyish face. He looked right past

Melody at Clark, who was doing an impression of someone deep in conversation on the phone.

She cleared her throat. "Um, hi. Good morning."

The man glanced down blankly at her. "Hey, how's it going? Good morning." His accent was French crossed with California surfer dude.

Melody peered into his eyes long enough to take note of what color they were. Greenish gray. "Hi," she said again, with what she hoped was a flirtatious and not a creepy smile.

To her surprise, the dark-haired chef's slow smile bloomed to full strength. "Hi," he said again, his gaze resting on Melody's face as if this were the first time he'd seen her standing there. "I'm Jerome. Nice to meet you." He reached forward to shake her hand, his eyes now locked on hers in a more-than-friendly way. "And you are?"

"Melody."

"That's beautiful name. A song." He let go of her hand but not her gaze. "I haven't seen you here before. Are you the new cowboy? Too lovely to be a cowboy, I think."

Flirting wasn't something that Melody had a lot of experience with. Jerome's attention made her warm and jumpy, but so did the thought that Clark was eavesdropping and watching her every movement. A hot blush rose up her neck, but she didn't break eye contact. "I'm just helping out today. Clark mentioned your name once. Are you a chef? At Le Monarque?"

Her simple question unleashed a friendly, animated monologue in which Jerome explained his role as a chef, the difficulty of finding good kitchen staff, the challenges of running multiple kitchens at once, the unpredictability of diners and the cruelty of restaurant critics. Crowds funneled through the farmers' market and still Jerome talked while his staff waited patiently like horses tied to an invisible hitching post. At one point, gushing about organic produce, Jerome reached into one of the crates on his cart and pulled out a perfectly ripe white peach. He took a small folding knife from his pocket and cut a thick wedge for her.

"Taste that," he said, holding the blade up to her mouth. The fruit resting on the metal glistened wetly in the sunshine.

Melody took the piece of fruit with her fingertips and ate it. It was sweet and succulent. The bite was slightly too big and juice dripped out of the corner of her mouth. Jerome stared at her lips as she wiped away the liquid with her fingertips.

"Gorgeous," he murmured. He was leaning forward slightly, looking down at her through narrowed eyes. "God, I've never wanted to be a peach more in my entire life."

Before Melody could respond, Clark suddenly appeared at her side. Slipping his phone into his pocket, he grabbed Jerome's other hand and shook it hard, dislodging the tiny hearts in the Frenchman's eyes.

"Hey, Pepé Le Pew," Clark said, overloud.

"How's it going, bro?" Jerome said, the spell broken. He folded the knife and put it away.

"How's the food truck? Everything on schedule? Have you thought more about our last conversation?"

Confused, Melody looked back and forth between the two men. They yukked it up like old friends, and Clark stepped out of the booth in order to talk to Jerome out of her earshot.

Lucky climbed out of the van and elbowed her in the ribs. "Look at you. Man-eater," he whispered.

"I'm not sure what just happened." She felt light-headed. The flavor of ripe peach still lingered in her mouth.

"Powerful voodoo magic, that's what just happened. Clark's voodoo."

The quivery feeling in her stomach made her wonder if Lucky was right—maybe Clark was using magic. Or maybe Clark had played a prank on her. Either way, she didn't like magic and she didn't like pranks. As Clark talked to the chef, Melody and Lucky helped customers. In between buyers, Melody thought she caught Clark watching her over his shoulder. But when she blinked, he'd looked away and she had to convince herself she was seeing things.

"I feel really loopy today," she said to Lucky quietly. "Maybe I'm getting sick."

"Just a few more hours, Mel. Then it's home sweet home."

* * *

After the long drive back to Oleander, Melody kicked off her sneakers and lay down on the ancient couch in her family's double-wide trailer. She needed a nap. Now that it was summer vacation and she was on break from teaching English at the local middle school, she helped shelve books at the college library. This third job with Clark was helping to pay off the used car she'd just bought for her little sister. With a deep sigh, Melody closed her eyes and dozed off.

When she opened her eyes again, it was dark. Harmony stood over her dressed in a sparkly minidress and heels. A ring of keys dangled from her finger, and she was jangling them like jingle bells.

"Mel, you promised!"

Melody groaned. Seven years younger, Harmony was a good girl, studious and hard working, but she could be a colossal pain in the devil's ass sometimes.

"What did I promise you now?" Melody rolled over and covered her head with a throw pillow.

Harmony yanked the pillow off her sister's head. "You promised to be my designated driver. Tonight. It's my graduation party at the Silver Spur. Everyone's going to be there." She grabbed Melody's ankles, dragged her sideways and dropped her feet on the ground. "It's bad enough I have to throw a party for myself...and now my sister, my one and only living blood relative in the whole wide world won't even take me to my own party... Mom and Dad are rolling over in their graves. 'Why, Melody, why don't you love your sister? She's so good! Like an angel! *Ay, nako Diyos ko!*" Harmony mimicked their mother's singsong accent as she threw out the Filipino exclamation.

"'Like an angel'?" Melody threw the pillow at Harmony. "The only reason you want to go to the Spur is to rub yourself on a bunch of drunk cowboys. Mom and Dad would be so ashamed."

"Me-el!" Harmony bellowed. "I'm going to be late to my own party! Wash off the dead cow smell and come out with me!"

"Jesus Christ, I've been babysitting you my entire life," Melody grumbled, but she sat up and stumbled to the bathroom to take a shower.

"Don't worry. I'll be out of your hair in a couple of days!" Harmony called as Melody turned on the water.

The old pipes whined and rumbled. "I'm putting one of my dresses on your bed. It'll make you look like a girl. Remember that, Mel? When you took the time to look like a girl?"

"Must be all that time I now waste working three jobs to pay your nursing school bills." Melody got into the shower.

"For which I'll forever be grateful." Her sister's hand popped out from behind the shower curtain holding a new razor and shaving gel.

Melody groaned and took the instruments of torture. "Do I *have* to?"

"For me, yes!" Harmony called through the steam. "And when you come out, I'll do your hair and makeup. Hurry!"

An hour later, Melody watched as Harmony two-stepped into the Silver Spur where a group of her nursing school friends waited at the bar. The old honky-tonk was bustling, jukebox jumping while a live band set up their gear. Wall-to-wall butts and buckles filled the space from the front door to the pool tables. The only lights in the bar were the pinks and blues of the neon beer signs and the spotlights on the stage.

Someone vacated a seat at the other end of the bar. Melody hopped on, adjusting her short skirt as she crossed her legs. As much as she didn't want to admit it, her sister was right—it had been a long time since she'd dolled up. She wasn't wearing anything glittery and tight like Harmony was, but the black dress was breezy, short and low cut enough to be enticing. Harmony had curled her hair and applied some mascara and lip gloss. Melody fidgeted with her clothing and hair as though she were wearing an ill-fitting disguise. But one-and-a-half gin and tonics later, Melody had settled into the energy of the crowd. Three cowboys and a city boy had hit on her, and all four looked sufficiently crestfallen when she turned them down with a polite smile. She was here to watch over her little sister. Harmony was getting absolutely shitfaced, laughing her head off and playing an endless game of spin the bottle without a bottle. Melody needed to be the guardian tonight.

A little romance for herself? Out of the question.

As Melody watched the cowboys and cowgirls hooking up on the dance floor, the feelings she'd been bottling up inside started to leak out. Her father, who'd worked as foreman on MacKinnon Ranch, had died of a heart attack when she was only nine—she had few memories of him. But her mother had died only eight months ago, quite suddenly, from pneumonia. The fresh ache of losing her mother snuck up on her every now and then, curling around her like a quiet, malevolent animal that sucked all the breath from her lungs.

When her mother passed away, Melody had been living in San Diego with her long-term boyfriend.

When she told him she had to move back to her tiny hometown in the Central Valley to help support her sister and take care of her mother's affairs, Scott used the move as an excuse to finally end their relationship.

They'd had their problems. But Melody hadn't anticipated the finality of the breakup. So swift and clean. It was as if their eight years as a couple had never existed.

With a grimace, Melody swallowed down the last of her gin and tonic. One of the bartenders whisked her glass away and asked if she wanted another. Even though she did, Melody shook her head.

Something touched her bare arm. A warm fingertip grazed her skin from elbow to wrist. She looked up.

"Lost in thought again?" Clark leaned close and kissed her cheek, just as he had hundreds of times before. One of the Silver Spur's waitresses put a beer down in front of him and flashed a sexy grin. He smiled at the woman briefly and turned his attention back to Melody.

She shook her head. "It must be hard to be you."

"Why do you say that?"

"Women. The endless parade of women fighting for your attention."

"Oh, it's not so bad." Clark took a sip of beer.

"Where are all your brothers? They usually help carry the burden."

COWBOY PLAYER | 17

"I'm on my own tonight," he said. "But let's talk about you, not me. Why so blue, Mel? Baby sister all grown up?"

They turned to look at the crowd in front of the stage. Harmony had found herself a cowboy admirer. The lucky fellow was holding her close and nuzzling her neck as he led her around the dance floor.

Was Melody sad that Harmony was growing up? No, not exactly. Nostalgic, more like—for a version of herself she wasn't sure ever existed. Had she ever been that young and optimistic? Had she ever let herself be that free?

"I'm proud of her," Melody said at last. "It's been hard. Seeing our mom get sick like that. Lots of kids would've dropped out. But she finished school with a 3.8. This is her first night out in a long, long time."

"A smarty-pants, just like you."

"Smarter than me," said Melody. "She learned something useful. Solid paycheck, helping others, all that good stuff."

"You're a brilliant teacher, from what I've heard."

"Diagramming sentences isn't exactly going to save us from the zombie apocalypse, now is it?"

"If there's a zombie apocalypse, nothing will save us, Mel. The only thing left to do is get drunk and screw." He held up his beer mug and winked at her. An honest-to-goodness wink.

Melody shook her head. "You can't help yourself, can you, MacKinnon? You're a hopeless flirt."

"Flirting? Thought I was just drinking beer and being myself." He looked down at the empty coaster in front of her. "What about you? What are you having? Gin and tonic, right?"

He remembered her favorite drink. Melody smiled. "No, I'm good. I'm on sister watch tonight. She really wants to cut loose. Someone's gotta hold her hair back when the vomit flies. Which it inevitably will." She waved her hand at him. "You should go have a good time. Get yourself a nice piece. Enjoy your Saturday night."

Only Clark could make a shrug look so sexy. "But I'm already enjoying my Saturday night."

Something about the way he said those words made Melody's skin tingle.

As an experiment, she uncrossed her legs and leaned forward, resting her arms on the bar. For a nanosecond, Clark's dark eyes darted to her cleavage before resting on his beer. A sudden, electric thrill shimmied down her spine. Her body clenched with pleasure, knowing she could still get the attention of a man as insanely hot as Clark MacKinnon.

But then…guilt.

That's Clark. Don't flirt with Clark.

The band started playing something loud and rowdy. Clark leaned forward. As he spoke into her ear, his warm breath caressed the sensitive skin on her neck. "You know, Lucky's going to be doing the rodeo circuit soon. It'll be just you and me on the road. Hours and hours together. You ready for that, Mel?"

Melody cleared her throat. *Be cool. Make a joke. Keep your distance.* "You and me and a couple hundred pounds of raw meat? Sounds kinky, Superman."

In the crowded bar, Clark stood flush against her, his arm pressed against hers. The sleeves of his dark T-shirt molded to the broad muscles in his biceps. Where the cotton ended, his skin was smooth and hot. She'd spent enough time with Clark shut up in the van to know he smelled pretty good—soap and leather, a little drugstore aftershave. Up close was a different story. That familiar smell, mixed with the subtle scent of his skin, made the transmission fall out of Melody's self-control.

"I had a feeling you might be kinky, Santos," he said.

He moved even closer. With gentle fingers, he brushed her long hair away from her neck and tucked the curls behind her ear. Intentionally or not, his bottom lip brushed her earlobe as he whispered, "Am I right?"

Christ. Heat rushed like quicksilver to her core, leaving her fingers and toes tingling with cold. She hadn't been this turned on in months, maybe years. Under the bar, she pressed her thighs together to ease the hot ache that Clark had summoned with nothing more than a few whispered words and the caress of his fingertips.

"Clark, what are you..." She trailed off and looked into his eyes.

Was he teasing her? Was he serious?

She and Clark had played in the creek together as little kids and slammed each other with dodgeballs in the schoolyard. She'd spent years in his company and yet, she couldn't remember what color his eyes were. Here in the neon light, she couldn't see his irises. But she could feel the unfamiliar heat of his gaze burning her like a thousand suns. Coming from a friend or lover, that look meant desire. That look meant sex.

The band finished the song with a loud holler and a wild drum solo. The crowd cheered. Clark locked his eyes on her for a half-second more before Tom Shelton, the big, tough-looking bartender, set down a row of shot glasses on the bar in front of them.

"Hey, Clark. Hey, Mel." Tom proceeded to fill the shot glasses from a bottle of cinnamon-scented whiskey.

Clark blinked and looked up at Tom. Melody folded her hands and rested them on her knees to keep from trembling.

"Your brothers here tonight?" Tom asked Clark.

Clark cleared his throat and shook his head. "No. All of 'em are busy."

"That's a first. How about you? What are you two up to?"

"Just keeping an eye on Mel's little sister."

"No kidding. She's a live wire," said Tom. "These shots are for her group, matter of fact."

Melody leaned back and glanced at the bar where Harmony's friends were sitting, but her little sister wasn't there. Melody looked back at the dance floor. Harmony and her new cowboy friend were nowhere to be seen.

"Clark." She hopped off the barstool. "I've lost sight of my sister. Can you see her?"

A full foot taller than Melody, Clark stood up straight and scanned the crowded room. "She was right there a minute ago."

"Ah, Christ," Melody said.

"We'll find her. She can't have gotten far." Clark grasped Melody's hand in his. With a warm, steady grip, he led her through the crowd, cutting a path for her. Together, they searched the dance floor and the area by the pool tables. They walked down the hallway leading to the restrooms and the smoking patio—still no Harmony. They were almost to the parking lot when Melody saw a flash of glitter in the corner of her eye.

In the darkest corner of the bar, tucked into a booth, Melody's baby sister was straddling a cowboy and sucking his face off like a lamprey on a dead flounder. The cowboy's big hands gripped the backs of Harmony's bare thighs and together they looked like they were doing a very private dance in public.

"What the hell!" Melody exclaimed. "Harmony!"

Harmony popped up, surprised. Her lipstick was smeared across her mouth and one strap of her dress hung off her shoulder. "Holy shit, Mel!" she exclaimed. She looked between Melody and Clark and after a couple of seconds, began to giggle. She was drunk as a skunk. "You two look like you've seen a ghost."

"Yeah, the ghost of my sister's dignity." Melody went over and adjusted Harmony's dress. "Get up. We're going home."

"What? Why?"

"Why? Because drinking is fine. Dancing is fine. Having sex in public? Not fine." Melody grabbed Harmony's wrist and pulled her to her feet.

"Easy now," Clark said softly. He took Harmony's elbow and helped her get her balance.

Melody looked into the dark booth to see who'd taken advantage of her sister. "You've got some nerve. She's wasted. I have a mind to call the cops on you."

The guy held up his hands. "Please don't call the cops." His words were slurred. He was as drunk as Harmony. "I just did what Clark said to do and the next thing I know—"

Melody knocked the hat off the cowboy's head to get a look at his face. "Holy fuck! Lucky!"

He blinked. "I'm so sorry, Melody. We just got carried away."

Behind her, Clark let out a hoot. When Melody glared at him, he pressed his lips together, but his eyes were still laughing. "No harm done, Mel," he said, holding Harmony up as she swayed on her feet. "Come on. Let's get these two train wrecks home."

* * *

Harmony passed out somewhere on the way between Lucky's house and the trailer. When they got home, Clark carried Harmony into her bedroom and lay her down in her pink ruffled bed. As Clark looked at Harmony's swimming trophies and first-place ribbons from science fairs, Melody removed her sister's endless jewelry: hoop earrings, jangling bracelets, rings. Each cheap metal piece clanked into the porcelain bowl on the nightstand.

When she came to, Harmony sang Carrie Underwood songs in between sighs and dreamy murmurings about what a blast the party had been. She began to complain that her sister was no fun, and why did Clark have to be such a stick in the mud tonight of all nights? All the girls said he was a good time. Apparently all the good times were done now that Clark was old. Ancient. As old as Melody, her sister who was as boring as all get-out.

Melody tucked the pink comforter under Harmony's chin. "Because you're being unpleasant, I'm going to leave your makeup on your face." She kissed Harmony's forehead. "I hope you break out."

"You're a mean old lady."

"Duly noted."

Clark brought a glass of water from the kitchen and an old pink crazy straw he'd found in the drawer. Melody held it up to Harmony's lips and made her little sister take three big gulps of water.

"I don't want any more."

"I don't care what you want. You're going to drink this so that you don't dehydrate and wake up hungover."

When Melody and Clark walked out of the bedroom and closed the door, Harmony was already snoring.

"She'll be in bad shape tomorrow." Clark sat down on the sofa. He took off his hat and ran a hand through his thick, dark hair.

"At least her first day of work isn't until Monday." Melody turned on the lamp, suddenly shy even though she had no reason to be.

"You know, I don't think I've been inside your house since high school."

"It hasn't changed much."

Clark looked at the old turntable across from the couch. Next to it, a glass-doored cabinet held hundreds of LPs. "Damn," he said. "Were all those your mom's?"

"Mom's and Dad's, all mixed together. Play whatever you want, make yourself comfortable—you want a drink?"

"What do you have?" He took off his boots, got up and opened the cabinet.

"Tanqueray."

"No beer?"

From the kitchen, Melody watched him as he looked through the records. "Nope. And you heard Harmony. You used to be fun. One cocktail. I know you can handle it."

She was squeezing lime wedges into two gin and tonics when George Strait's voice flowed deep and smooth from the old speakers of her parents' record player.

"Nice choice." She walked into the living room and handed Clark his drink.

"Classic." He was sitting cross-legged by the record player, looking at a dozen albums fanned out on the carpet in front of him. "They were like pieces of art, weren't they? Cardboard cover, liner notes. All the lyrics. We're never going to have this kind of thing again. Everything's digital. There won't be any hard proof of the music we listened to."

"Maybe that's a good thing." Sitting down on the sofa, Melody took a sip of her drink and ogled the curve of Clark's broad back, the way his muscles stretched his cotton T-shirt, showing off the hard contours of his body. He was a looker. Always had been.

"Maybe so." Clark examined the covers one by one. "Buck Owens. Merle Haggard. Great stuff. How did your parents become fans of country music?"

"My dad was born in Oleander just after his parents moved here from the Philippines. He started listening to country on the radio when he was a kid working in the fields. My mom was born in the Philippines. He loved the music and she loved him, so it made sense that she'd grow to love it too."

"They loved the music enough to call you Melody and Harmony."

"Thank God we weren't boys. What would they have named us?" She grinned to herself. "Buck and Merle. Hee and Haw."

Clark turned and looked at her with a crooked smile. "Twang and Yodel."

"Ooh, that's good. Twang Santos, Esquire." She took another sip and slipped off her shoes. "Dr. Yodel Santos."

"Paging Dr. Santos. Dr. Yodel Santos."

They snickered, fifteen again and goofing off in the back of geometry class. Still smiling, Clark gathered up the vinyl records and carefully returned them to the cabinet before sitting down beside her. He held his drink in his left hand and draped his right arm on the sofa behind her. She could feel his fingers stroking her hair. Intentional? Not intentional? All she knew was that his touch made her scalp tingle down to the roots.

"You know, I really am glad we're working together, Mel," he said. "Having you around—it's going to be a big help once Lucky's on the road."

She grimaced, remembering the sight of her sister riding her way to glory. "Ah, God. Lucky. Why'd my sister have to choose Lucky? Have you seen that boy tie down a calf? He's got the fastest hands in the county."

"I know you care about Harmony, but I wouldn't worry about it too much. They're both adults. Sometimes these things happen."

Spoken like a true player. Melody took another drink as she felt her heart hardening in her chest. For a moment, she wondered if Clark were the kind of man who could walk away from a woman the way her ex-boyfriend had walked away from her. "Sometimes these things happen," he'd say, riding off into the sunset and leaving a trail of broken hearts in his wake.

The image annoyed her enough to make her rude. "So that yoga goddess at the market today—was she something that happened to you?"

Clark looked at her and raised his eyebrows. "I'm a gentleman, Mel. I don't kiss and tell."

Melody blinked. "You did, didn't you?"

He shook his head with a smile. "You're too much."

"Was she good?" Another sip. "She looked like she'd be...limber."

Clark took his first sip of the drink sweating in his hand. "She was," he said quietly. "But that was the only thing she had going for her, unfortunately."

"I knew it!" Melody exclaimed. "What about the fisherman's daughter? Or the lady who sells flowers? And the coffee chick with the nose ring? Or that pastry chef who buys all those flats of berries?"

Clark let out a sigh.

"Come on. Just tell me," she said, nudging him with her elbow. "We're friends."

"All right. Fine. Don't repeat this to anyone." He counted them off on his fingers. "Yes, yes, she likes you not me, and yes."

"The coffee chick likes me?"

"A lot. Huge crush."

"Huh." Melody looked up at Clark. "Jesus. It's like there's this whole world of sex going on beneath the surface. Is there a secret portal or password or some kind of key I can get hold of?

"You want in, Santos?" He smirked at her. "I got your key right here."

Jesus Christ, that smirk should be illegal. "I'm immune to your charms, MacKinnon."

"That so?"

Her cheeks were warm. From the flirting or the gin? "Yup," she said, meeting his gaze. "Like a little clownfish in the gooey tentacles of a sea anemone."

"Really? Let's test that theory out." He put his glass down on the coffee table, wiped his hands on his jeans, and climbed on top of her. Straddling her legs with his thick thighs, he put on a duck face and began to do a goofy lap dance, gyrating his hips like a stripper.

She couldn't help it. She began to laugh. "Oh my God. Cut it out, you perv."

He put both hands behind his head and began to undulate his torso. "Feeling tingly yet? Has paralysis set in?"

Giggling, she tried to push him away without spilling her drink. "No, but you're giving me the heebie-jeebies."

"I fuckin' love it when you talk like my nana, Mel. It's so sexy in a deeply twisted, Freudian way." He began to hump her knee. "Tell me you're wearing granny panties. Whisper it in my ear."

She put her hand on his chest and tried to wiggle away, laughing too hard to be turned on. "I can't imagine how other women resist you."

"Me neither. It's never happened before." Grinning, he put his big hands on her shoulders and kissed her cheek. On the record player, the next track started. Guitar licks, drums, a little fiddle—Melody knew the song at once.

"Oh man," said Clark. "'Troubadour'. This a good one. Dance with me, Mel."

He pulled her off the sofa before she could say anything. Wrapped up in the arms of a big cowboy was not a terrible place to be, so Melody danced with him, barefoot in her parents' living room, the slow two-step a song both their bodies knew the words to. Her laughter died away, giving way to a quiet sense of vulnerability. The verses slid by like a dream, erasing the burden of loneliness she'd been carrying for so long. It had been months since she'd been this close to a man. It had been years since she'd *felt* this close to one.

Clark could read her mind. "So what was his name again?" he asked softly. "Scott?"

"Yeah."

"What happened?"

"A slow-motion disaster, that's what happened." She rested her cheek against the hard, hot wall of Clark's chest. "He was a musician. Fun. Exciting. He said I meant the world to him. But I suppose the world wasn't enough."

"What do you mean?"

It was still hard to say aloud. "He cheated on me. It had been going on for months. When I found out and confronted him about it, he broke down said he was sorry. We tried to put it past us. We even went to therapy. But it was all a lie. He left me when my mom passed away." At first, the pain had been excruciating, dulled only by grief and the weight of her new responsibilities. "Eight years, down the drain."

"That's a long time. Did you ever talk about getting married?"

"He said he didn't like labels." She sighed. "Which was also a lie, because he married the other woman in Vegas in February."

"Jesus Christ. I'm sorry." Clark gave her a squeeze. "You know, if you were mine, I'd hold on to you for good."

"Sure. Until the next piece of ass came along."

"Never seen a piece of ass like yours."

"That's the friend talking. Your dick might say otherwise."

"My dick, huh?" Clark laughed quietly. "You're welcome to check with my dick yourself. He doesn't talk loud, so you'll have to get down on your knees to hear him."

"Jackass."

"Seriously, Mel. You don't know what you've got going on. Smart as all get-out. Hell, you run circles around me, and I'm a genius. And you're funny too. Ain't many women who can make me laugh. You're one of them."

She rolled her eyes. "Aw shucks, Ma. Next the cowboy told me I was real purty."

"Fuck pretty. You're beautiful."

It was too much. *Danger.* "Clark—"

"So beautiful. I always thought so." He gave her a sad smile. "Honest to God."

The heat rising between them cooked her brain. She was at a loss for words. "Thanks."

"No thanks needed. Just stating the obvious." They danced until the song ended on a ribbon of steel guitar. Clark leaned down and pressed his lips to her temple.

Melody gasped.

Instead of pulling away, he traced a slow, agonizing trail of kisses along her hairline until he was kissing her neck just behind her ear.

Pleasure overloaded her nervous system, but her brain wouldn't let her enjoy it. "Wh-what are you doing?"

"Something I've wanted to do for a long, long time."

"Oh God." She gripped his rigid arms. Complicated feelings cascaded through her so quickly, she couldn't identify one from the other.

Still holding her, he looked into her eyes. "Don't be scared," he whispered. "Look at me."

For the first time in twenty-eight years, she realized Clark's eyes were brown. No—not brown. Swirled mahogany and gold, like bird's-eye maple, with irises rimmed in dark chocolate. Her body ached under his warm gaze, ravenous for what he offered her but terrified of what they'd lose if she took it.

"We're friends," she said. "I don't want to throw that away."

"Nothing will change that." He searched her face. "Do you think I'd hurt you?"

"Not intentionally." Loneliness welled up inside her. Her heart was a broken bucket at the bottom of a deep well. "And I know what it's like when you think you know someone, and then you discover..." She trailed off.

"But you know me," he said. "I'm not hiding anything. You know me better than anyone, right?"

She nodded.

He was quiet for a moment. "One night's not forever, Mel." The expression on his face was unreadable. "We're adults."

"Yeah, but—"

"Tell me you don't want this. Tell me no."

She closed her eyes. Could she? Should she? Lust flooded her bloodstream. "What if...I don't want to tell you no?" she whispered.

He pressed his body against hers. At once she felt his desire for her, hard and real and burning against her belly.

"Then tell me yes," he murmured.

Desire trumped fear. She wanted this. She wanted him. Melody took a deep breath and opened her eyes. "Yes."

Clark had big hands. One big hand cupped the back of Melody's neck. He put two fingers under her chin and raised her head to meet his gaze. With a touch as gentle as his voice, he stroked her bottom lip with the tip of his thumb.

"Just to be clear, Melody," he whispered, "I'm asking to take you to bed. Is the answer still yes?"

If the devil looked at her like that and asked for her immortal soul, she would still give the same answer: "Yes. God, yes."

Then Clark kissed her.

Six foot two, hard edges and curves, thick limbs and broad shoulders and big muscles—it seemed odd that he'd have lips as soft and full as the ones he pressed to hers. Melody's eyes fluttered closed as the man she saw as the definitive player kissed her as shyly as a teenager. The shape of his mouth melded sweetly to hers as his fingertips massaged her nape. Bit by bit, her conscious mind surrendered to the sensations. The warmth of his skin. The faint smell of gin on his breath. The sweet flavor of his mouth when, after what seemed like an eternity, he parted his lips and stroked the tip of her tongue with his.

And all was lost.

Melody reached up and ran her hands through his dark, soft hair as Clark slid his hands down her back. At once the gentle kiss became wild. She could feel him breathing hard as she opened her mouth wider to let him in. Their tongues entangled, Melody began to tremble, unable to process the tremendous intimacy of what they were doing. When she gripped his shoulders, he broke their kiss at last and with a sharp intake of breath, kissed her neck, sending delicious shivers up and down her spine. Her body felt at once both tight and loose—a bundle of tension, slowly warming and softening like molten metal under his touch.

His hands slid down lower. His cupped her ass in his enormous hands and pulled her hard against him. She heard a low groan in his chest that reverberated against her solar plexus.

"Christ," he whispered against her throat. "Up. Get up."

She reached up, wrapped her arms around his neck and, when he grabbed the backs of her thighs, hopped into his arms. Short but by no means tiny, Melody felt self-conscious for only a moment until she realized that Clark was a milk-fed farm boy. She'd seen him wrestle his brothers. She'd seen him pick up and throw down two-hundred-and-fifty-pound calves. The man was as strong as an ox, and in his arms, she felt safe. He gave no indication that she weighed anything at all.

"Wrap your legs around me," he said.

She did. Every part of him was hard and lean. Between her thighs his torso was rigid as concrete. As he looked up at her, the words tumbled out before she could censor herself.

"You're one handsome motherfucker, you know that?"

"Glad you think so."

He carried her to the sofa and let her down gently. As he knelt between her legs, Clark pressed soft kisses on her cheeks, her closed eyelids and her forehead. Then his kisses grew more wicked. He covered her neck with long, hot breathy kisses until Melody was sure her blood had turned to lava in her veins. He kissed her throat as he grazed the insides of her bare thighs with his fingers. He French-kissed her madly, eyes wide open and filled with gleeful challenge. And Melody, ignited with lust, had to face a strange fact—making out with Clark MacKinnon was not only taboo and hot as hell, it was fun.

She leaned back. "Take off your shirt," she whispered.

Slowly, he grabbed the neck of his T-shirt and drew it over his head.

Jesus Christ on a motorbike.

Melody was sure she'd seen him shirtless before. Probably at the lake, on someone's houseboat. At a barbecue, pitching horseshoes. Maybe on the ranch. But the difference between seeing and *seeing* couldn't have been more real than it was in this moment. Clark was like a beautiful book that had sat on her shelf for years that she'd never bothered to take down and read.

Broad shoulders capped with muscle. Rounded pecs and pale-brown nipples. His brothers were all big hairy bears, but Clark's chest was nearly smooth, with just a light dusting of soft hair that trailed down between the aggressively carved muscles of his six-pack. His shallow belly button—almost an outie—made Melody smile. At the waistband of his jeans, deep lines of muscle peeked out above his hips. Constellations of tiny moles and freckles covered his ripped torso, beautiful imperfections.

Captivated, she reached forward and touched him. His skin was hot. When her fingertips grazed his abs, he took her hand before she could go any lower.

"Not yet."

He grabbed her by the waist and drew her down lower on the sofa until her hips were flush with the edge of the cushions. As he kissed her again, Melody felt his fingers pressing against the under curve of her breasts as his thumbs slowly, agonizingly circled her nipples through the fabric of her dress and bra.

"God, I need to see you," he said against her lips.

He slid his hands underneath her dress and pulled the fabric up. Melody sat up as he removed the dress from her body, reached behind her and unhooked her bra. He set her back down and looked at her almost naked beneath him, his eyes wide and his jaw tight.

"Gorgeous," he whispered.

More kisses. Her lips grew swollen and tender. His five-o'clock shadow abraded her chin and cheeks. Clark kissed a wicked trail down her throat between her breasts as he stroked her areola with the warm pads of his fingers. Just as she began to squirm, his hot mouth closed over her right nipple. As he suckled her, she threaded her fingers through his hair, pulling gently as a long, low moan escaped from her throat. Then he moved to her other nipple and did the same thing. When he rubbed the heel of his hand against her through her panties, bright pleasure swirled in her brain. When he slipped his fingers behind the lace and ran his fingers over her wet, slick flesh, her eyes shot open and she gasped.

Clark flashed her a smile as he reached down and slid her panties down her legs. He threw them onto the sofa by her head, put his hands on her knees and drew her legs slowly apart, spreading her wide.

"Do you know how long I've fantasized about this?" He touched her again, drawing his fingertips slowly from the bottom of her pussy up to the tip of her clit. "When you left for college, I thought I'd lost you forever. And then you came back."

Melody could barely register the words. "What?"

Without saying anything else, Clark lowered his lips to her and with his hot tongue, followed the same trail that his fingers had just taken. Melody gasped and grabbed on to the sofa pillows. This was unreal.

Barely breathing, she watched as Clark pressed his rough cheek against her inner thigh and looked at her. His warm, gentle breath on the most intimate part of her body. His eyes rested on her, scorching her like fire. With his fingertips, Clark stroked her tender pussy, parting the petals of her sex with his thumb and forefinger, exposing her clit. His lips were an inch away. Anticipation intensified the ache inside her, a longing so strong her skin grew feverish.

"I need you, Mel," he whispered, lowering his lips.

The first licks were like wildfire, so pleasurable they were almost painful. Clark closed his eyes and Melody could see the shadows of his eyelashes on his cheeks. With each hot caress of his tongue, she could sense him feeling out her reaction, learning what she responded to, memorizing what she liked. It didn't take him long to find his rhythm. Melody shut her eyes and began to breathe harder as all the blood in her body rushed to meet him, her heart pumping furiously in her chest.

Her ex-boyfriend had stopped going down on her years ago. For as long as she could remember, her only real orgasms were the ones she gave herself alone in bed or in the shower, furtive, shameful ones that were her only relief against the intense loneliness to which she'd resigned her life.

She thought she was the only one who could make herself feel good.

She was wrong.

For a long time, Clark licked, caressed and sucked her. From the way he moaned and stroked her thighs and looked up at her reactions, he was enjoying himself. His wicked tongue never left her body. Her body drew so tight she could barely breathe. He had taken her to the edge of climax and back twice before she realized that her hands were cramping up from holding on to the sofa so tightly.

With a smile as naughty as it was beautiful, Clark lifted his head and looked up at her.

"Amazing," he said.

He stroked the drenched folds of her pussy, then slowly slid a finger into her. He drew it in and out, massaging her and stretching her gently. When he slid in a second finger, she gasped and clenched at him, hard, a monster of an orgasm threatening to break free.

"Ready?" he whispered.

She nodded, unable to speak.

Clark closed his eyes and dove in. With the tip of his tongue, he swirled her clit with perfect pressure and perfect heat. He did it again and again and again, relentlessly, as his fingers thrust into her, stretching her tight. The mixture of pleasure and pain destroyed her resistance.

"I'm going to come," she whimpered. "Oh God."

She arched her back hard and the climax tore out of her, rushing through her nervous system and lighting up her spine like a roman candle. Goose bumps broke out all over her body, and her nipples hardened to tiny, erect points. The convulsions in her pussy were so strong, so endless, she wasn't sure if she was having one orgasm or twenty. All she knew was that Clark had done this to her. Clark her buddy, Clark the player, Clark who was kneeling between her thighs wearing a smug grin, his dark eyes shining with nothing short of pure delight.

When the climax finally receded and Clark removed his cowboy Casanova fingers from her person, Melody lay back on the sofa, a hot and panting mess. The needle on the record player chuffled rhythmically against the label, the music long done. It was the first time she'd noticed the sound. Her body was on fire, scorched from the inside out by the biggest orgasm she'd ever had in her life.

"What the fuck, MacKinnon?" she said, staring up at the ceiling.

Clark laughed softly as he kissed her forehead. "You ready to have that conversation with my dick now?"

CHAPTER TWO

The Player

Strange what desire will make foolish people do.

—CHRIS ISAAK

H *ell yeah.*

She came. He'd made her come.

"What the fuck, MacKinnon?" she said, staring up at the ceiling.

Clark laughed softly as he kissed her forehead. "You ready to have that conversation with my dick now?"

The joke hid the rawness in his chest. She was more beautiful than he could've imagined. Golden-brown skin, smooth as a dream, covered her tight, compact body. Her sexy hips and full breasts enticed his eyes and hands, and even now, after feasting on her, his mouth watered for more of the sweet sexiness between her legs. The way she moved, the way she moaned his name, the way she came—she was everything he desired in women wrapped up in one woman. Melody.

"Come on." He helped her to her feet.

"God, I hope Harmony didn't hear anything," she whispered. "Let's go."

She grabbed her clothes and turned off the record player. As he followed her down the dark hallway, Clark rubbed the aching erection in his jeans and tried not to feel a pang of annoyance. Who cared if Harmony heard? Who cared if anyone heard? He was tired of keeping his feelings a secret.

The truth?

He'd been in some form of love with Melody Santos ever since his little-boy heart could wrap itself around the concept of love.

Years and years ago, when his dad's best friend and ranch foreman died of a heart attack, Dale MacKinnon had promised to keep an eye on Nicasio Santos's widow and two daughters. Which meant that at every birthday party, every First Communion, every Christmas and Easter for as long as he could remember, Clark ran around the ranch not just with his brothers, but with Harmony and Melody too.

Harmony was always too young to do much of anything but get in the way, fall down and be the reason everyone else got in trouble. But Melody was a different story. She and Clark were the same age, and she was a tough cookie. She roped and rode and wrestled. She wasn't afraid to get dirt on her church clothes or mud on her fancy shoes. Clark loved to play pranks on his brothers, and Melody was always his willing assistant, a source of misdirection and distraction for his victims. When the pranks were done, he made sure she never got in trouble. She never did.

In school, they were always the brainiest kids in the room, but Melody always got the answers a split-second before him. Then, sophomore year, something changed. He started growing taller. And he didn't stop. His older brothers, heartbreakers and jocks, had generously prepared a reputation for him to inherit. Girls—lots of them—started to show interest in him. When they started showing interest in what was in his pants, he obliged them.

These girls came and went. But Melody was his best friend. She bullied him into Academic Decathlon. She enrolled him in advanced placement classes without asking him first.

And senior year he realized something—he was in love with her, and not just in the way a magician loves his assistant for making his illusions look good. He wanted her. Alone, in the shower particularly, he often liked to fantasize about the moment when—if she ever became interested in such things—he could show her what was in his pants.

Clark never asked her out, a chickenshit move that he regretted to this day. They graduated before he worked up the nerve. He got into the local state college to study farm management and business. She got a scholarship to a fancy university in San Diego to study education and English literature. And just like that, his one constant was gone.

He'd lost her.

Until now.

She didn't want a relationship—fine. He was never any good at boyfriend-girlfriend stuff anyway.

But hell if he was going to let her go tonight.

Melody led him into a small bedroom, closed the door and turned on a bedside lamp. As she stashed her clothes in the closet, Clark noticed that the room was nearly empty. The outlines of paintings and picture frames marked the walls. The only furniture was a big bed, a nightstand stacked with books and two cardboard boxes marked Goodwill.

"Tell me if you're cold. I can switch the heater on," she said softly.

As Melody turned down the covers, a quiet realization settled over him. She'd moved into her mother's old room. How much grief could one woman process at one time? The loss of a long-term relationship. The loss of her mother. Melody had taken on the task of looking after her sister with such grace and strength, it was easy to forget the burdens she was carrying.

Clark went to the bed and stood behind her. She was still gloriously naked. As he ran his hands slowly over her bare arms, her smooth skin puckered under his touch. When he began to massage the tension out of her shoulders, her head fell forward and she let out a soft sigh.

He leaned down and whispered, "I'm not cold. Are you?"

"No," she said, turning around.

When she got up on her tiptoes to kiss him, Clark closed his eyes and savored the feeling of her soft, full lips on his. She tasted cool and sweet, like the limes she'd put in their cocktails. As she kissed him, her hands roamed his body, stroking his neck, his shoulders, his back and his arms. She pressed her breasts against his chest, and he swore he could feel the sizzle between them like drops of water on a hot griddle. He pulled her close, and she jumped in surprise, recoiling a little.

"What?" he asked.

"Your belt buckle. It's cold."

Before he could say anything, she dropped to her knees and undid his belt and the buttons on his fly. Together, they pulled down his jeans and his drawers at once. He danced out of his socks and kicked everything out of the way. Eyes wide, Melody slid her hands down his sides, resting her cool palms on his hipbones.

Finally free, his cock rose up toward her, aching and wet at the tip.

Oh God. Yes.

"So this is what all the girls talked about when we were back in high school," she said, looking up at him with a sly smile.

He grasped the base of his cock and stroked himself slowly. "I didn't know they talked."

Melody raised a skeptical eyebrow at him. "They did. And I heard."

"Once you heard, did you ever wonder?" He was finding it hard to keep his cool. He was hard as fuck, and the head of his cock was a half-inch from her lips.

She gave him a half shrug. "I didn't think it was right, wondering about my best friend's dick."

He slid a hand over his aching balls. "Is it right to wonder about your best friend's pussy? Because that's what I was doing."

"Liar."

"God's honest truth, Mel. I had the biggest crush on you." I still do.

She rolled her eyes. "When did you ever have time to have a crush on me? During five-minute breaks between banging everything with a smile and a snatch?"

"Hey now," he said, stroking her hair. "Why don't you put that sassy mouth to use?"

With one sideways glance at him, she took his wrists and moved his hands away. When her soft fingers encircled his shaft, he almost collapsed forward with pleasure. When her pillowy lips closed over the head of his cock, a strangled groan jumped out of his chest.

"Jesus Christ," he whispered.

Like everything she did, Melody gave him her all. At once, she slid her mouth down as far as she could go, pushing the head of his cock into the deepest part of her throat before drawing him slowly back out. Massaging his exposed shaft with both hands, she did this again and again, pausing only to lash the underside of his cock with dozens of hot, sweet licks that set off fireworks of pleasure all throughout his body, from the bottoms of his feet to the tips of his fingers.

"Look at me," he said, stroking her cheeks.

Full of silent laughter, she looked up at him with her enormous dark eyes. She blinked once, twice, then slid off his cock and went to town licking and sucking his balls, which had tightened up against his body, threatening to blow and embarrass him in front of the woman he'd been in love with for almost all of his life.

"Stop, stop," he hissed. "Ah, fuck."

He grimaced, all of his energy going to denying himself an orgasm. Hot, translucent drops of precome fell on her chest, sliding down between her breasts. He stared at the sight, transfixed, as she smirked at him like some kind of wicked wet dream.

"You okay, MacKinnon?" she said, teasing him.

He closed his eyes and regained control. When he opened them again, a deeper hunger took over than the one that had brought him to her bedroom in the first place. He wasn't just in love with Melody. He was in love with who he was when he was with her—strong and potent, just like her.

He reached forward, grasped a handful of her silky black hair, and gently but firmly pulled her head back.

"You okay, Santos?"

Something shifted in her eyes. Her playfulness disappeared at once, replaced by something else. Something he knew well. Lust. Hunger.

"Open," he whispered.

They stared at each other, both knowing that something had forever changed between them. When she opened her mouth, he took a moment to look at her. This woman had haunted him for so long he'd come to accept that she'd always be a ghost in his life. But here she was. So real, so beautiful and so vulnerable that touching her almost hurt.

Still holding her hair in one hand, he grabbed the base of his cock and slid himself into her open mouth. She looked up at him, hypnotized. He drew back and slid forward, thrusting against her tongue until he was deep enough that his balls grazed her chin. The supplication in her eyes set his blood on fire, as did the eventual realization that while he fucked her mouth, Melody was stroking herself, her fingers working between her legs until he could hear the wetness of her arousal.

His body ignited. He began to sweat. This was the fucking sexiest thing he'd seen. Ever.

Carefully, he put his hand under her chin and pulled himself out of her mouth. He let go of her hair, bent down and kissed her, a long, hungry kiss that reflected the scorching knowledge that had just risen between them.

She likes it dirty. Just like me. Hallelujah.

Clark picked her up and laid her on the bed. He grabbed the condom in his jeans, ripped it open and slid it on. In a second, he was kneeling on the bed between her open legs, staring down at her, his heartbeat in his throat.

"You ready?" he said softly.

"I think so," she whispered. Worry shadowed her expression. "You're really big."

He nodded. "We'll go slow."

Clark took himself in his hand again and leaned forward. Slowly, he dipped his tip between the drenched folds of her pussy, then pulled out and circled the wet head of his cock around her swollen clit. Pleasure dripped like hot morphine through his veins. He repeated the motion once, twice. Each time he did it, Melody's nipples hardened and her chest rose and fell with deep, frantic breaths. So he did it again. And again. When he did it the sixth time, he leaned forward and gave each of her tender nipples a long, hard suckle. She moaned his name, and he almost came again.

Get it together, Clark.

He braced himself above her and moved his hips until the head of his cock was lodged inside her. She squeezed him and he swore his balls kicked themselves. Clark's nerves were shredded. This would be over too soon if he didn't concentrate. He clenched his jaw. This shouldn't be happening to him—he never lost control in bed.

"I feel like I'm gonna die if I don't feel you all the way inside me." Her voice was the faintest whisper above his ragged breathing.

"Now?"

"Now."

He locked his eyes on hers as he pushed himself forward into her in one slow, agonizing thrust. The resistance of her body combined with her hot slickness lit up the highway between his cock and his brain. He'd just dipped his cock in nirvana.

When he was halfway inside her, she clenched up and whimpered. He froze, responding to her pain.

"Ease up. Breathe, Mel." He balanced on one forearm and licked his thumb. "Shh."

He reached down and slid the pad of his thumb up one side of her pussy where it was stretched taut around his cock. Gliding upwards, he found her tender clit and with the gentlest pressure, began to stroke her.

Melody closed her eyes and dropped her head back on the mattress. "Oh God."

Clark pulled back and pressed forward, a little at a time, while she grew wetter and wetter around him. He kissed her neck, assaulting her sweet spots with his tongue and lips, even grazing her skin with his teeth. The moment she stopped bearing down, he lifted himself up on his arms, swung his hips forward and drove the length of his cock into her. She stifled a moan and dug her nails into his back. It was the best kind of hurt.

"Clark," she whispered. "I can't believe this is happening."

He got control of his breath. "I know."

She was drenched. Her clit was slick and stiff against his thumb. He dragged his shaft out and thrust again, watching her face to gauge her reaction. Her lips parted. Her neck went slack. Only her eyes were shut tight, crinkled up with tension.

"Look at me, Mel."

She opened her eyes. Up close in the soft lamplight, he saw the galaxies swirling in her dark brown irises, that familiar filament of copper like a lightning bolt straight to his heart. He could close his eyes and picture hers as clear as a photograph. He'd memorized them when he was seventeen years old.

He began to make love to her, slow, deliberate thrusts that knocked the words out of his brain. She arched against him and spread her legs wider, rising to meet him. He was hot—so hot. Their bodies began to glisten with sweat in the cold bedroom and the sound—God help him—the sound of him fucking her filled his ears. He replaced his thumb with his forefinger, pressed down gently on her clit and began to rub her just as he'd done with his tongue. Her pussy grew even wetter. She grabbed the bedsheets.

"Oh God."

She came in a furious, sudden shudder, the convulsions massaging the length of his cock from tip to root and back. A whispered torrent of swear words and gibberish poured out of her mouth. She drenched his hand and the front of his abs in a filthy, sexy baptism. Clark had never seen anything like it.

Not waiting for her to finish, he sat up and tucked his shoulders against her calves. Leaning deep against her thighs, he cupped her ass with his hands and lifted her an inch off the soaking sheets. The angle gave him full access to her tight little body.

"I've fantasized about this for so fucking long," he growled.

Her eyes were wild. "Then do it."

Clark took one last coherent breath and slammed into her, balls-deep. His brain shut down. He became an animal, driven by a desperate need. He pounded into her. He dripped sweat on her. Pleasure overloaded his nervous system.

The springs in the ancient mattress began to chirp like a flock of birds. Riding on a wave a mile high, Clark leaned forward, bending her into a sharper angle that left her completely vulnerable to him. She closed her eyes and tightened around him, her smooth inner muscles crushing the last of his control.

The room pitched. He threw his head back. Every muscle in his body flexed. An orgasm too powerful to be real ripped through him, emanating from the molten-hot point where his body joined hers. He was going to die—death by an overdose of pleasure, injected straight into his bloodstream.

When he was coherent again, he opened his eyes. He'd collapsed onto her, still inside her. She was stroking his cheeks. Her face was wet with sweat and tears.

He panicked. "God, did I hurt you? Are you all right?"

She smiled and sniffled. "Shh. You didn't hurt me. I'm fine." Her eyes were luminous as she ran her fingers through his hair. "I don't know what to say."

Clark blinked at her, just as speechless. Sex this wild—it didn't happen between friends. It didn't happen, period. He wiped her tears away with his hand and did the only thing that made sense. He kissed her again.

* * *

A strange muffled sound roused Clark from a deep sleep. He opened his eyes. He was in an unfamiliar room in an unfamiliar bed. A sleeping girl was nestled against him, soft and warm. Her gentle breaths stirred the hair on his arm where he held her in a tight embrace. The memories of what they'd done the night before came to him slowly, like a remembered dream.

Melody. He sighed. Fuck yes.

Under the blanket, he had a boner the size of the Washington Monument.

Blue light filled the room. It was early.

And then he heard the sound again—the buzzing of his phone on the carpet. He willed it to go away. It did. Then it started right back up again.

Probably important. Stifling a groan, Clark gently untangled himself from the beautiful sleeping woman, stumbled into his jeans and picked up his shirt and the phone. He stepped out of the bedroom and closed the door silently behind him.

In the living room, he answered the call. It was his youngest brother, Caleb.

"What?" he whispered.

"Jesus God, finally."

"What do you want?"

"Where are you? I need the truck. I gotta take Mom and Dad to Bakersfield."

"Where the hell's your truck?" Clark buttoned his fly and buckled his belt.

Impatience flared in Caleb's voice. "Dean has it again. He's doing some work at the Singh place."

A chronic problem. Too many brothers. Not enough trucks. "Then use the van."

"Godfuckingdammit, Clark, the van won't start. You run that thing into the ground."

Clark sat down on the couch and sighed. "Is Dad okay?"

"He hasn't felt right since his last chemo session on Tuesday. Mom wants him in urgent care."

"All right. I'll be there as soon as I can."

"Hurry."

Clark hung up. When he looked up, he almost jumped out of his skin.

"You two tie one on last night?" Looking like the devil hocked a loogie on her, Harmony stood at the kitchen counter. She wore an old pink bathrobe with cows and crescent moons on it. She tore open a packet of Alka-

Seltzer and dropped the tablets into a mason jar filled with water. "That couch is uncomfortable as hell. You should've just crashed with my sister. She wouldn't have cared." Harmony watched the trails of bubbles then looked up and winked at him. "My bed's comfortable too. I wouldn't have cared either."

Clark gave her a half-smile. She was a hot little mess but nowhere near as sexy as her sister. He shook out his T-shirt and put it back on. "You are a passel of trouble, ain't you, Harm." He got his boots on, located his hat and headed for the front door. "Listen, tell Melody I have to go. I'll call her this afternoon."

"Will do, Superman."

* * *

Clark gassed up the truck and drove it home. After he showered and changed, he picked up his phone. He was about to call Melody when his brother Dan cracked the whip.

"You're late for chores. Let's go." Dan tossed him a pair of work gloves.

For many years, Dan and Clark, the middle MacKinnon brothers, had worked the ranch under their father's supervision. Now that their old man was sick, it was up to them to run the show. Together, they managed employees, ran operations and handled all of the accounting decisions that made the ranch a viable business. They faced a lot of challenges. This year's drought was bad. Both brothers worried that the pastures wouldn't be healthy enough to support their stock.

After six hours working outside and three hours in the office, Clark was dusty and ill-tempered. It was early evening. One of their crew members was butchering some meat to sell at tomorrow's farmers' market in Santa Barbara. Clark would have to check in with him to pack the coolers and double-check the inventory. After that, he'd have to figure out what was wrong with the van. He'd be lucky to be done by seven.

The office was tucked behind the mudroom of the farmhouse. Dan had already gone home to his wife and kids, who lived in their own bungalow a five-minute walk away.

Clark leaned back in his chair, stretched and yawned. He'd been up late with Melody. They'd gotten three, maybe four hours of sleep. He smiled to himself, remembering what they'd done instead.

Feeling giddy, Clark pulled out his phone to call her. When he tried to start it up, he realized it had died—he hadn't charged it last night. He went upstairs, plugged it in and turned on the screen.

Three missed calls from Melody, no messages, no texts.

"Shit."

He let the phone ring until her voicemail picked up. He cleared his throat, feeling weird even though he called her all the time.

"Hey, Mel. It's me. Sorry about this morning. My folks needed the truck and then I was out all day with Dan. I didn't get your calls until now. My phone died because I didn't charge it..." He trailed off, suddenly afraid that he sounded like he was making excuses for running out on her. "Anyway, I'll try calling you again later tonight." He paused, not knowing what else to say. "I hope you're all right. Okay. Bye."

After inventory, Clark and Dean jump-started the van and let it run. Caleb and his parents got back from the hospital a little before eight. Dan's wife made a late dinner for everyone, but Clark's father went straight to bed. By the time dinner and clean-up were done, Clark was bone tired. After another shower, he collapsed on his bed and checked his phone. One text from Melody.

Call me. I'll be awake.

Her phone rang three times before she picked it up.

"Clark."

"Hey." Clark put a hand behind his head and looked up at the ceiling, a warm feeling settling in his chest at the sound of her voice. "How are you doing?"

She was quiet for a moment. The silence that stretched between them didn't feel awkward to him. The universe was stretching to accommodate this new thing they'd become. Not friends, not lovers, but something deliciously in between. His body began to tingle. No longer tired, he entertained the thought that he could get dressed, hijack the nearest truck and be back in her bed in about thirty minutes. Who needed sleep, anyway?

"Listen," she said. "I have something I need to tell you."

"What's going on?"

"I won't be going to Santa Barbara with you and Lucky tomorrow. I can't."

He sat up. "Is everything okay?"

"Yeah, yeah. Everything's okay." He heard her lick her lips. He wished he were there to do that for her. She continued, "Actually, I won't be able to go with you to farmers' markets any more. At all."

"What? Why not?

"I talked to Tom Shelton this afternoon. He's willing to take me on as a cocktail waitress at the Spur. I start training tomorrow at eleven."

"What are you saying?"

"I have to drop my job with you. I'm sorry, Clark."

He could sense her skittishness. She was a horse about to bolt. "Wait. Wait right there. I'm coming over. Let's talk in person." He stood up and looked around his room for a clean pair of jeans.

"No, no. Don't do that. Don't come over."

"This—you and me—this has nothing to do with our working relationship. I never meant—"

She cut him off. "This new job—it pays a little more. I had to put down a deposit on my sister's new apartment in Bakersfield. We still have the costs from my mom's memorial. And I need to get ahead of Harmony's student loans. It'll be a while yet before she's making enough to start paying them off herself."

"If money's the issue—"

"It is an issue." She let out a breath. "But it's not the only issue." She paused. "Clark, I can't do this. I can't go down this path again."

"What do you mean by 'again'? I'm not your ex-boyfriend. I'm not Scott." He made a fist and tapped it softly against the wall. "You know me, Mel. I'd do anything to keep from hurting you."

"I know. I just need a little space," she said quietly. "After some time, maybe…maybe we can be friends again. Maybe we can come back from this."

Maybe? "Is this because I left this morning? Mel, I had to go. Caleb needed the truck to go to the hospital with my folks. The other stuff, it just piles on top. On the ranch, there's just no way to get out from under it, you know that."

"I know. I know that you have a lot of responsibilities."

"Jesus." Clark sat back down on his bed. He never let himself get close to other women like this. Never close enough to get burned. Now he knew why. Powerless, he grasped at words, not sure what he was saying. "I'm serious. I won't hurt you. I'm not like your ex-boyfriend. I swear."

"This situation is just too complicated for me right now. I've got a lot on my plate."

Her broken heart, her mother, her sister and their bills—Clark knew the battles. He had no intention of adding to them. "Let me help you. Let me stand by you. I'm not going anywhere."

"Like you said, I know you. You don't do relationships. Never have." Her voice wavered. "And I don't want to be that annoying woman who forces you to pretend to be someone you're not. You'd come to hate me."

"Mel, come on."

"Besides, you said it yourself. 'One night's not forever.' Right?"

He cursed under his breath. He'd tossed that line out there because he was dying to go to bed with her last night. Sometimes he couldn't believe the stink of his own bullshit. "You're looking for reasons to run away," he said slowly. "If that's what you really want—"

"Yes. That's what I really want." Her voice broke. "Good-bye, Clark."

And just like that, she hung up.

Clark lay down and looked blankly at his phone. He never realized that such a banal object had the power to crack open his rib cage and incinerate everything in his chest cavity like napalm.

* * *

Two weeks passed.

Lucky never asked why Melody stopped doing the farmers'-market runs with them. In Oleander, the grapevine had great reception. Clark just assumed Lucky'd heard the whole story or some version accurate enough to know that Clark didn't want to talk about it. So they didn't.

On the ranch, Clark worked with his brothers and spent time in the office feeding spreadsheets and running reports. As he expected, Melody didn't call or text. After a dozen calls, he gave up.

With each passing day, he was becoming a moody asshole. Dean, his oldest brother and the moodiest asshole in the family, even remarked on it one afternoon while they were doing some yard work for their mom.

"You okay?" he asked.

Clark shrugged. "Yeah. Why?"

"You don't seem like yourself."

"Like myself? How?"

It was Dean's turn to shrug, cowboy-speak for you know how. Out loud, Dean said, "Want to grab a beer at the Spur?"

"I thought you were hanging out with the Singhs again tonight."

"I am. That's why I said a beer and not some beers."

Clark had been avoiding the Silver Spur. He didn't know which nights Melody worked, so it made the most sense not to go at all. "Maybe another night," he said.

"Suit yourself." One last shrug from his brother meant that the conversation was done but a point had been made. Clark had to shape up. In his very laconic way, Dean was right. What happened happened. Clark couldn't change these circumstances. He'd just have to get used to the new order of the universe and maybe the big sucking wound in his chest would eventually heal up on its own.

The next morning, Clark had just gotten off the phone with a bank about a loan application when his cell phone rang.

"Hey, bro, long time no see."

French surfer-dude accent. Clark smiled. "Hey, Jerome. How's it hanging?"

"Loose, bien sûr."

They talked a little about Jerome's restaurants and all the recent foodie buzz in Los Angeles and San Francisco. Jerome's publicist had gotten him a spot on a local TV news program to promote the food truck. Jerome was thrilled to be making his Hollywood debut. He was contemplating getting a new tattoo.

Then he said, "Clark, my friend, I have a problem."

Clark's ears perked up. "What's going on, bro?"

"Beef. Beef is my problem." Jerome made a sound, halfway between a tsk and a hiss. "I'm having trouble with my supplier. He's in Northern California, and he says the drought has damaged his pastures to the extent that he needs to dry lot his animals. I can't go with that product. Not with my restaurants. And especially not with this new food truck—burgers made with 100 percent grass-fed beef is the whole concept."

Now Clark's radar was spinning. He and Dan had done everything they could to keep their pastures healthy. If he could secure a contract with Jerome, MacKinnon Ranch would be in the black at last. "Tell you what. Email me some numbers," he said cheerfully, even though adrenaline was pumping through his veins. "Let's see what we can do."

"I can do you one better," said Jerome. "Prepare some reports for me. Come to Le Monarque tomorrow night. Stay at the Hotel Roxbury. My treat. Come have a night on the town and let's discuss this tête-à-tête."

Le Monarque was Jerome's fine-dining restaurant in the Hotel Roxbury right above the Sunset Strip. It was one of the hottest celebrity hangouts in Los Angeles.

"Are you serious?" Clark asked. "You don't have to do that."

"No, bro, I want to. You would be helping me out of a jam if this works out. As a matter of fact, bring your hat. They'll think you're John Wayne." He laughed. "Oh. And you know what? Why don't you bring your friend too? The cowgirl, I think her name was Melody?" Jerome cleared his throat. "Out of curiosity, is she seeing anyone?"

"Seeing anyone? Ah, no, man," Clark said, stumbling over the words. Jerome was trying to sound casual about Melody, but Clark could tell he'd been thinking about her. "Melody...she's single. As far as I know."

"Great! Fantastic. Bring her." In the background, Clark heard a crash of dishes and an explosion of cuss words in three languages. Jerome groaned. "Okay, my friend. Gotta go. Seven o'clock at Le Monarque. Tell the hostess you're my guests."

Clark ended the call. He was alone in the office, so no one saw him put his head on the desk and give it three gentle thumps. A pencil rolled off the edge and landed on the floor.

"Shit," he whispered.

* * *

Clark had never noticed that the cocktail waitresses at the Silver Spur wore uniforms until he saw Melody wearing hers. Cowboy boots, cut-off jean shorts and a plaid shirt tied up at the waist—the Daisy Duke special. Clark contemplated sending the owner Tom Shelton a thank-you note.

Melody stood at the till adding up a bar tab. Shapely legs, a slender waist, softly muscled arms, and high, round breasts. There was a silvery scar on the back of her left thigh where she'd fallen while riding his horse—they'd been twelve at the time, and Clark had been racked with guilt for months. Just above her rhinestone belt, faint stretch marks striped her lower back. She hated them; they started showing when she was about seventeen. These so-called flaws made her even more beautiful to him. Years of shared history meant that he could read her body like a book.

The room was less than half full. Another cocktail waitress sat at the bar chatting with Tom. Slow night.

Clark took a breath. Do it.

He walked right up to Melody and leaned against the bar. "Don't rabbit," he said quietly. "I have to talk to you."

She was wearing more makeup than usual. It was an alluring look, but he knew that she was even lovelier without the war paint. Her fingers flew over the touch screen. She didn't look him in the eye. "I'm at work. We can't do this here."

"This won't take long. Just listen."

As quickly as he could, he laid out the scenario with Jerome. A half-dozen emotions danced across her face as he spoke, but none of those emotions were positive.

"Let me get this straight. You're asking permission to pimp me out to your friend in order to secure a contract," she said. "That's really classy, Clark." The receipt printer got jammed. She had to open it and unspool the paper.

"Jesus. Stop." Clark stood up straight, nudged her out of the way and began to work out the paper jam. "You've seen our numbers. The ranch is in trouble. The drought. My dad's hospital bills—insurance doesn't cover every-thing. If I sign Jerome, the ranch's finances will be solid for the first time in years." He shut the cover and the printer screeched into action. "If you're there he'll be more relaxed. More likely to make the deal. I'm not pimping you out. I'm asking you for help. As a friend."

She tore off the receipts and grabbed a pen from her apron. "Then as a friend, I say no. I've gotta work."

Clark waved to the other cocktail waitress. The blonde bombshell sashayed over.

"Rhiannon," he said, looking from one woman to the other. "You working tomorrow night?"

"No." Rhiannon leaned languidly on the bar. She had hazel eyes, but her left iris was slightly lighter than the right. "Whatcha have in mind, cowboy?"

"Could you cover a shift for Melody?"

Rhiannon raised her eyebrows, mildly offended. "What?"

"I'm trying to fix Melody up with a friend," he said quickly. "I'd owe you big time, Rhi."

The woman smiled. "All right, Clark. I'll do it. For you." She looked at Melody. "And get this darling girl laid, will you? She's been moping around here for days." With a wink, Rhiannon turned and left.

Melody looked up at Clark and shook her head. "I need that money, you know."

"I'll pay you."

"You can't afford to throw wages around like that."

"If we sign Jerome, I'll pay you double what you would've made on that shift." He searched her face. "What do you say?"

"You get women to do your bidding all the time, don't you?" She sighed and shifted her weight from one leg to the other. "Okay, Clark. One night." She stuck a finger in his chest. "But I'm doing this for your brothers and your folks, not for you."

"Yes! Thank you, Mel." He almost leaned forward and kissed her, but he stopped just in time. He glanced at himself in the mirror behind the bar. A big goofy grin sat on his face. He turned back to her. "So you've been 'moping around'? Interesting."

Melody did not return his smile. Instead, she brushed past him, tray under her arm. "You should go. I've got to get back to work."

* * *

Clark was in so far over his head, he might as well have been standing on the bottom of the ocean.

First of all, the woman was going to kill him.

High-heeled silver sandals, curled hair, makeup— Melody had put on the dog, and she smelled like apple blossoms in the Garden of Eden. Worst of all, she wore a dark-blue handkerchief that some highfalutin' fashion people called a dress. On the two-hour drive to Los Angeles, she wouldn't return his attempts at conversation. So they sat in silence, Clark slowly crumbling in the presence of so much rampant sexiness.

Second of all, this place.

Jesus.

The Hotel Roxbury stood on a small side street above the Sunset Strip. Built sometime in the 1920s, the old chateau-style hotel radiated Hollywood history. Perfectly clipped high hedges surrounded the property, hiding the luxurious cars that entered and exited the grounds. When they pulled up to the entrance in Caleb's jacked-up old Silverado, Clark took the ticket from the valet and led Melody inside. Her heels clicked over the polished

Spanish tile in the cavernous lobby. A bellboy collected their overnight bags and handed them their room keys. They didn't even have to stop at the front desk.

Feeling like an oil baron, Clark snapped the kid a five-dollar bill. Melody hid her smile and automatically took the arm he offered her.

"What?" he said.

"Nothing," she said. "Let's go."

The entrance to Le Monarque was tucked in the back of the lobby. An orange-stained glass monarch butterfly decorated the restaurant's door. A sedate, well-dressed crowd stood three deep at the bar. Dozens of people crowded the hostess stand, waiting for a table.

The hostess looked up when Clark approached. When he tipped his hat, her eyes widened, then narrowed and got sultry right quick. She had bright green eyes, like a Heineken bottle. Melody's grip on his arm grew just a shade tighter.

"Evenin', miss," he said, turning up the twang. "Clark MacKinnon and Melody Santos. We're guests of Jerome."

The hostess nodded. "Good evening," she said. "Follow me, please."

They bypassed the bar and the crowded dining room. The hostess seated them in an enormous semiprivate booth bathed in candlelight. A big picture window faced the courtyard where twinkle lights dangled from jacaranda and date palms. Spotlights lit the enormous stone fountain in the center of the gardens.

"Your server will be with you in a moment. Chef Dupont will be joining you for coffee and dessert." The hostess nodded to both of them, her gaze lingering on Clark. "Enjoy your evening."

When they were alone, Melody fidgeted in her seat, scanning the space. In the candlelight, her golden-brown skin glowed and her dark eyes sparkled like polished obsidian.

"Beautiful," Clark murmured. He wasn't referring to the restaurant.

She nodded. "Amazing."

They didn't have one server—they had a team of servers. Jerome had prepared a tasting menu for them along with wine pairings for every course. The fanciest restaurant Clark had ever been to offered all-you-can-eat breadsticks, so the spectacle of flavors overwhelmed him. By the time his steak arrived, there were ten different glasses on the table. He wasn't sure if he was supposed to drink from them or play "The Sugar Plum Fairy" on the glass harp.

His steak—well, that was pretty good. Jerome had chosen to serve Melody a whole lobster. Clark's nose wrinkled at the ostentatiousness of it all. Damn Frenchie. He sliced off another hunk of meat and shoved it in his mouth. Showoff.

"You okay?" Melody asked when the servers were out of earshot.

Clark swallowed. "Yeah. Sure. Why wouldn't I be okay?"

"Because you look like you're about to go on the warpath." She lowered her voice and leaned toward him. "Are you worried about the contract? Is Jerome interested in a supplier for only the truck or for all his restaurants?"

"He was pretty vague over the phone. But I want it all. All five of his restaurants plus the truck. Rumor has it he's opening up a place in Las Vegas next year. Big and splashy. I want in on that too."

"You sound confident."

"You're here. I feel confident." He looked at her, afraid she'd retreat from him again. "I don't mean that the way it sounds. What I mean is, I'm glad you came. Thank you, Mel."

Looking a little uncomfortable, she lifted her wineglass. "Hardest shift I ever worked, boss."

The meal waltzed forward, each course punctuated with another glass of wine, a bite of sorbet, or something small and strange perched on a porcelain spoon. By the time dessert rolled around, Clark was buzzed on wine and Melody's company. He was afraid he might be blushing. His brothers used to tease him that he blushed whenever he was embarrassed or drank too much.

Shape up, tough guy, he thought to himself, loosening his collar.

Suddenly, Jerome appeared and slid into their booth next to Melody. He was wearing a black chef's jacket and his longish hair was tied back in a little ponytail.

"Hey, hey, my friends." A bright smile lit up his face. He shook Clark's hand and gave Melody a European kiss-kiss that made Clark's fists tighten under the table. "How are you, beautiful girl?" He spoke rapid French to the server, who quickly brought him an espresso in a tiny white cup, three bar glasses and a dark bottle.

Jerome reached forward and twisted the cap off. "Fernet Branca. Have you tried this? It's good, but a little strong."

The dark liquid tasted of heartbreak and Armageddon. But Clark smiled like it was pink lemonade and laughed when Melody made a face. "Aw, come on, Mel, it's not so bad."

They talked food, as usual. Jerome's philosophy of fine dining was to dazzle the senses and to create a spectacular experience. He walked them through each of their courses and told them that the lobster was from Santa Barbara, as was the sea urchin in their pasta course. Clark's steak was from the last of his old supplier's grass-fed herd.

"It was good," said Clark, "but we can do better."

Jerome laughed. "Ah, the cojones on you, cowboy. I admire that. I admire that, bro."

Clark reached into his jacket to take out the reports he'd prepared.

But the chef held up his hand. "Hang on a second." He called over the server again. More French. The server nodded. Jerome turned back to Clark. "This gentleman will escort you to the office. My accountant and sous chef are waiting there. Let's make the deal tonight, what do you say?"

Stunned, Clark put the documents in his jacket pocket, stood up and put his hat back on. "I say that sounds pretty great." He shook Jerome's hand again. He turned to Melody. "Ready? Let's go get those papers signed."

The chef stayed seated, blocking Melody's exit out of the banquette. "Actually, I was hoping to get a little more acquainted with your friend here," Jerome said, eyebrows raised. "You know. Enjoy our coffee. Take a walk around the grounds." He looked past Clark at the server and nodded again.

"Sir, if you'll just follow me," said the man.

Clark made eye contact with Melody. She lowered her chin almost imperceptibly. Go ahead, she seemed to say. I can handle him.

"Okay." Clark tried to keep his voice cheerful even though every protective bone in his body wanted to grab that bottle of Armageddon and smash it over Jerome's ponytailed head. With a phony smile, Clark said to Melody, "I'll meet you in the lobby tomorrow at nine, all right?"

She nodded. "I'll be there."

"Okay," he said again, feeling like an idiot. "Have a good night, you two."

He could hear them whispering to each other as he entered the dark hallway that led to the kitchen. Then he heard something that crushed his nerve and sent him into full-blown jealous asshole mode.

Melody's laughter.

God, he missed that sound.

* * *

A king-sized mattress, a down comforter, ten thousand thread-count sheets, enough feather pillows for twelve heads. Didn't matter. It was still the most uncomfortable bed Clark had ever slept in. He rolled around for hours, trying to find a position that didn't feel wrong in every way.

With a sigh, he sat up and turned on the lamp. The room was luxurious and beautiful. He didn't want to think about how much it cost. But that was what happened when you were part of the Jerome Dupont team.

Gold rained down from the sky and everyone got to eat well.

The deal was better than he could've imagined. He'd called Dan as soon as the contracts were signed. In the background, his sister-in-law and the kids cheered and banged on pots and pans. When Clark arrived home tomorrow, he'd talk to his dad. The old man had always advised Clark that selling directly to restaurants or individual consumers always made more sense than selling to any processing plant—it just took more work. And today, Clark's work paid off.

So why did he feel like a piece of shit?

He checked his phone. Two in the morning. No texts, no messages from Melody. Before he'd gone to bed, he'd walked down the hall to her room to check on her. No answer.

Could she really take care of herself? Had he put her in danger? Jerome dressed like a biker, but he wasn't a fighter. Clark could tell—he'd been beaten up enough times to know when he could take someone and when he couldn't. And Melody was tough. She'd grown up with the MacKinnon boys, for Christ's sake.

But none of this rationalization made him feel any better.

The room was hot. He got up, pulled off his T-shirt and stepped out onto the balcony.

The cool night air embraced him. Bars and clubs were closing on Sunset Boulevard. A few drunk people wandered the sidewalks, talking loudly and laughing. A thin sheen of dew had formed on the metal railings of the balcony. Clark wiped his hands on his pajama pants and stretched. A few pushups opened up his lungs. Crunches and sit-ups got his blood pumping. As he did a few squats, he realized he wasn't used to eating like he'd eaten tonight. Maybe a run tomorrow would be good, after that long drive.

He had just drunk a glass of water from the sink in the bathroom when he heard a soft knock on the door. He opened it.

Melody was still in her dress, but she was barefoot. Her sandals dangled from one hand. There was a pink rose in her hair.

"Can I come in?" she whispered. Her eyes were puffy. She'd been crying.

Clark sat her down in the big plush armchair and brought her another glass of water. As he watched her drink, he made a very serious decision. He was going to kill Jerome tonight. He was going to kick the shit out of Jerome, and then he was going to deliver as many head shots as it took to separate the Frenchman's soul from his body. Quickly, he made peace with this decision. He'd sing Johnny Cash songs as they strapped him to the electric chair.

"What did he do?" Clark asked. He sat in front of her on the coffee table. "Tell me, Mel. We'll make this right."

"What?" Melody put the glass down. "What do you mean?"

"If he touched you—"

"Touched me? Jerome?" She looked confused. "No, he didn't do anything. We drank coffee and walked around the garden. Then he kissed me good night. That was it." She removed the rose from behind her ear and put it in the water glass. "Perfect gentleman, actually."

"Kissed you? On the lips? So help me God—"

"On the cheek."

"Did you give him permission? Because—"

"Clark, cut it out." She leaned forward. "Listen. I'm not here because of Jerome."

Now it was Clark's turn to be confused. "You're not?"

"No." Then her face crumpled. Tears began to pour down her cheeks.

At once, he gathered her up in his arms. In his ample experience, he found it was best to just let girls cry it out. Whenever he tried to say something to make them feel better, they tended to cry harder. So he shut up, stroked Melody's hair, made soft shushing noises and tried to hide the erection that had risen at once in his pajama pants.

When her tears ran dry—which took a while—he rocked her gently her back and forth until she was calm again.

"God, I've been so stupid." She sniffled. "I thought that if I pushed you away—if I was nasty and mean to you—you'd stop coming around and I'd stop thinking about you."

Clark's heart began to beat harder. "Did your plan work?"

"No. Not at all." She looked up at him. "I think of you day and night. I can't stop."

CHAPTER THREE

The Game

A wareness of the insanity of love has never saved anyone from the disease.

—ALAIN DE BOTTON

Melody didn't have a game plan when she knocked on Clark's door. If she'd taken the time to draw one up, she probably wouldn't be sitting on his lap now, streaming snot and spewing forth a babbling confession about how much she'd been thinking about him, day and night.

God. So cheesy. What are you doing?

She wiped her nose on her arm and leaned her head against his shoulder, emotionally defeated. She'd screwed this up big time. Nothing left to do but keep going. "When I woke up that morning and you were gone, I panicked. I immediately went to a very dark place. A place I thought I'd left behind once Scott and I broke up. I was pacing the house. Calling your phone and hanging up. Imagining the worst."

"Why?"

"I was afraid you never wanted to see me again. I was a wreck. I had promised myself I'd never be that person again. And there I was. Same as ever. Needy. Suspicious. Mistrustful."

Clark took her hand and squeezed it. "I should've told you good-bye before I left. That was a mistake."

"It was, but a small one. In my mind, it became this huge monstrous thing," she said. "Looking back, I hate the way I reacted. I was wrong. So wrong." She closed her eyes. A cold breeze blew in from the open balcony doors, but Clark's body radiated heat. Her skin tingled against his. "I'm so sorry. I'm sorry for trying to push you away. For what it's worth, I didn't mean any of it."

"You didn't?"

She looked up at him again. He sat still as she reached up and stroked his face, cradling his cheek in her hand. "No."

He closed his eyes and pressed his face against her palm. "I thought you hated me."

"No," she whispered. "I could never hate you." Melody felt many, many emotions for Clark MacKinnon, but hate was not one of them. When she kissed his cheek, he sighed and his body relaxed against hers, slack but solid with muscle. "I missed you, Clark. It's been a long two weeks."

He gave her a squeeze. "Yeah. It has."

They held on to each other in silence. The minutes ticked by and slowly, they began to breathe together, their inhalations in sync. Wrapped up in his big arms, she let Clark's warmth envelop her. Flashbacks of their shared passion lit up her nervous system like faraway lightning. He'd changed everything she'd understood about sex. He'd taught her things she didn't know about her own body. For days, he'd haunted her nights and waking dreams.

"I know you don't do relationships," Melody said softly.

"I would try it. For you."

"You don't want to get tangled up with me," she said, shaking her head. "I have serious trust issues. I'm poison."

"Jesus, stop it."

Fear, real and cold, cut through the warmth swirling in her chest. She'd never asked a man to sleep with her before. "I don't want to lose you as a friend," she said slowly. "But tonight, I can't help wanting..." She trailed off, unable to find the words.

They were quiet for a long time.

When he finally spoke, Clark's voice was deep and steady. "I think I know what you want, because I want it too." He stroked her hair and kissed her temple, the exact same place he'd kissed when he first invited her down this rabbit hole. "One last night together. Right?"

She gasped softly, relishing the sensation of his lips on her bare skin. Pleasure spiked in her brain like a drug.

"One last night together," she repeated. "Then we leave this part of us behind. It stays here and we move on. What do you think?"

He was quiet for a moment. He stroked her lower back, edging lower and lower with each languid sweep. "If this is going to be the last time I'm going to make love to you," he whispered against her neck, "I'm going to give you everything I've got. Are you ready for that?"

The sultry promise in his voice sharpened her senses. She was more than ready.

"Yes," she whispered.

His taut chest was feverish against her fingertips. She tipped her chin up, closed her eyes and kissed him. Their lips melded together so sweetly that the pleasure of it trickled like warm honey through her body.

Clark MacKinnon could kiss like an angel, but there was nothing angelic about the way he made love. As he kissed her, Clark untied the straps of her dress, pulled the silky fabric down and tossed it away. He unfastened her strapless bra and dropped it on the carpet. His big thumbs hooked on to the waist of her panties; when he yanked them down, Melody caught the scent of her own arousal. She was wet for him. She'd been turned on from the moment he'd answered the door, shirtless and hotter than the hinges on the gates of hell.

Clark ran a slow trail of kisses down her throat until he reached her breasts. He sucked one hard nipple into his mouth and teased her with the tip of his tongue. Then he reached down and put his hand between her legs. He swiped one warm finger from the base of her slick seam up to her clit. Melody hissed, unprepared for the shock of his touch.

"You okay?" he whispered, a wicked grin on his lips.

"I'm burning up."

"We can fix that."

He slid his arm under her knees and picked her up at once. Feeling lightheaded with desire, she wrapped her hands around his shoulders as he carried her to the balcony.

"Someone will see," she said.

"No one will see." He set her down. The clay tiles were cold against her bare feet, and the cool breeze raised goosebumps on her naked body. "Put your hands on the rail, facing me."

She did as he told her. The wrought iron railing was cold and she recoiled for a moment. He reached out and clapped her hands to the metal.

"I said, 'put your hands on the rail'," he growled.

The cool command in his words made them stronger than any rope. She shivered, remembering the night they'd slept together. His outward sweetness belied a man capable of making her come so hard that she'd felt echoes of his pounding deep inside her body for days.

One more searing kiss and Clark slid to his knees before her. "Open," he said.

Her breath in her throat, she spread her legs. With his giant hands, Clark stroked her hips with the barest touch before sliding the pads of his thumbs forward to part the dark hair just above her sex.

Her senses sharpened. She heard the cars passing quietly below on Sunset. Crickets sang in the shadows, a late-night mockingbird babbled in the eucalyptus trees. The seventh-floor balcony was dark. Clark was right—no one could see them.

Clark leaned forward and, without preamble, sealed his hot lips over her. His muscular tongue strummed her clit immediately, flicking it with a steady rhythm that matched the drumbeat in her chest. Her hands tightened their death grip on the rails. Each lash of his tongue amplified the lust coursing in her veins. Her ears filled with the wicked sound of his licking as he drew more arousal from deep inside her. Their first night together, he'd taken his time. Tonight, he had her number and there was nothing tentative about his intent.

Before she could register what was happening, Clark ran the tip of his tongue around the crown of her clit, then pressed down hard, sending jolts of pleasure to her brain. An intense orgasm seized her at once. Melody threw her head back and looked up sightless at the night sky as blood and dopamine coursed through her. Clark's tongue was relentless. He continued to lick and suck on her, drawing out her climax as she trembled and gasped. She'd never come so fast.

Without a word, Clark picked her up again and threw her over his shoulder like a caveman. He dropped her on the bed and, standing over her, took off his pants. Melody, still twitching, reached forward and slid her hand over his erection. He was hot and rigid. As her fingers trailed over him, she still had trouble reconciling that this big, perfect cock was attached to her best friend, the guy she'd grown up with.

His eyes blazed with lust. He grabbed her wrist and pushed her hand away.

"Not yet." The deep rumble of his voice washed over her.

He stroked himself as she watched. The slick tip of his cock swelled and his shaft grew darker and thicker. In response, her tender pussy clenched and grew even wetter. Her thighs were streaked with slickness.

"Touch yourself," he commanded.

Eyes locked on his, Melody reached between her legs and ran her fingers over the soaked, swollen lips of her pussy. Her clit was still tender from his tongue. Instead of touching it, she pressed the tip of her middle finger into her opening, then drew it out.

"Deeper," he said. He took his cock in his fist and began to pump harder. "All the way."

She did it. She was slick and tight. When Clark licked his lips, her smooth inner muscles tightened around her finger.

"Goddamn." He reached into the overnight bag by the bed and rolled on a condom. Then he sat down on the bed with his legs straight in front of him on the mattress. "Come here. Face the door."

Melody crawled to him in the dark. She climbed into his lap in reverse cowgirl. When his shaft brushed her inner thigh, she jumped as if he were made of red-hot metal. Clark put his hands on her waist and drew her back towards him. In full control of her body, he took his shaft and pressed the plump head against her opening. Then, again without warning, he grabbed her hips and thrust upward, impaling her on his steel-hard cock.

Christ.

The bite of pain. The agonizing stretching. The delicious fullness. He made small circles with his hips, working his way even deeper into her. They groaned in unison, ecstasy coming down on them like a hot drizzle from heaven.

"You are so fucking tight," he said. She pressed her lower back against his rigid torso. He reached up to knead her aching breasts in his hands. Melody hissed as he pinched her nipples—gently at first, then not so gently. "I thought about you. Constantly. Did you know that, Mel? Did you know how much I wanted you? I jacked off every night. I jacked off every morning. Like some kind of fucking teenager." He squeezed her breasts and thrust deep. She couldn't move, paralyzed by pleasure. "In fact, just like when I was a teenager. I jacked off for you back then too."

She pressed down on him and clenched her muscles as tightly as she could around his shaft. With a tortured groan, Clark let go and leaned back on the mattress.

"Ride me," he murmured.

Melody bent forward and balanced her hands on his shins. She raised her hips, sliding slowly up and down his cock, clenching on the upstroke like she was milking him.

"Yes," he whispered. "Like that."

When she looked over her shoulder, she saw that Clark's lips were parted and his eyes were narrow. He was staring at her, mesmerized. The expression on his face emboldened her, and she speeded up the pace. He groaned again and shifted his hands to her hips where he held her steady, adjusting her speed and depth as if she were his own personal sex toy. Melody was so aroused, she could feel her own wetness dripping all over his lower abs and thighs. Under her fingers, his skin was slick with sweat. Through the faint traces of his after-shave, she could smell the clean sweat of his body, a scent she'd forever associate with heat and lust. She rode him until they were both delirious.

"Does this feel good?" she whispered.

"Sweetheart, it feels amazing."

Sweetheart. She closed her eyes and relished the sound of that word coming out of his mouth. She'd never been anybody's sweetheart before.

"I think you need to fly again," he said.

He pushed her forward and she caught herself on her hands. She squeaked in surprise, but he caught her hips and raised them so that she could get to her knees. When she was balanced on all fours, Clark adjusted himself inside her, grabbed her hips once more and gave her a half-dozen slow, shallow thrusts, digging the head of his cock against a delicious place inside her. When he reached around and stroked her clit with the pad of his forefinger, Melody wailed with unrestrained pleasure.

"You like that, don't you, Mel?"

Her voice was broken. "God, yes."

He did it again. Six thrusts, all aimed with laser precision at her G-spot. His wicked finger swirled her clit. The delicious sensations overloaded her system. She could feel another enormous orgasm waiting in the wings, ready to come onstage and make her sing.

"Say my name," he said. The sweet man she knew was gone. In his place was this potent lover who turned her on in every way.

"Clark."

He pulled the move again. Six taps on her G-spot. The hot swirl of his finger.

"Say, 'Fuck me, Clark'," he demanded.

She was breathing so hard her mouth could barely form the words. "Fuck me, Clark."

He licked his thumb. When he brushed the ultrasensitive opening of her ass, Melody clenched up around his cock.

"Shh," he said. "Let me in. Just a little."

The strokes were featherlight, strange but hot as hell. Aroused out of her mind, Melody murmured, "Yes."

At once, Clark pressed in to the first joint of his thumb. He speeded up the strokes on her clit. When he hit her G-spot once more, Melody bore down involuntarily, then seized up and froze.

"Yes. Fuck yes," Clark whispered.

She clamped down hard on Clark's shaft. A full-body orgasm grabbed hold of her at once. She came so hard that she was screaming before she realized she'd made a sound. Clear, sweet liquid spurted out of her in time to the wild pulsations of her pussy. What had he done to her? This was more pleasure than she'd ever felt in her whole life, concentrated into a single beam of ecstasy.

Before she'd finished her climax, Clark withdrew his thumb and pushed down on the middle of her back until she was leaning on her forearms. Her face was nearly buried in the bedsheets, her back was arched and her ass was up in the air. He grabbed her hips once more and thrust again, this time with such force that she wailed again.

But Clark didn't make a sound. He slammed his cock into her over and over, withdrawing so far that every time he thrust forward, he seemed to go deeper and deeper. Her pussy stretched mercilessly around him. She would be hurting if not for the fact that she was drowning in her own arousal, her body slick from two orgasms and primed to take a beating. She grabbed handfuls of the bedsheets and braced her knees against the mattress. His grip on her hips tightened as he pounded her like an animal. But Melody relished it, this unleashed sensuality, this secret side of Clark that she didn't know existed. He was beautiful and frightening, as dark a lover as he was as bright a friend.

He was breathing through his teeth; his hot breaths cooled her sweat-damp skin. Three more deep thrusts and he froze, his rock-hard abs pressed against her ass cheeks, his balls cool and heavy against her clit.

Impossibly, he thrust even deeper and pinned her in place, the head of his big cock pressed up against a spot near her cervix.

Holy fuck.

Melody closed her eyes. Intense shockwaves of sensation gathered like a whirlpool inside her, as if he'd discovered a new G-spot at the very back of her pussy.

When Clark began to come, he pulled Melody into the gravity of his orgasm. She climaxed a third time, confused but too overcome with lust to care. Pleasure, heat, sweat and come—Clark and Melody tumbled together in the enormous wave, their time together as lovers dying one agonizing second at a time.

She fell asleep almost the moment he withdrew from her body. She woke again, just for a moment, when the bed dipped and he came back from the restroom after cleaning up. Reflexively, she reached for him and wrapped her body around his.

"Good night, Mel," he whispered against her cheek.

She breathed him in, drawing him into her dreams. "Good night."

* * *

Clark looked down at Melody. The pain he felt in his chest was at complete odds with the pleasure he felt everywhere else.

Who needs a fucking heart anyway?

Drowsy and lovely, she lay under him, her dark hair a beautiful mess on the pillow. Earlier, after they woke up in each other's arms, she didn't say a word when he reached down between her legs and slowly caressed her with his fingers until she was silky and hot again. She didn't say a word when he put on another condom. And she didn't say a word when he eased inside her, the morning sunlight filling her glistening eyes with fire.

Her fingertips drew wide, lazy circles on his back. She wrapped her legs around his hips and every time he thrust, she clenched at him, drawing him deeper into the dark mysteries of her body.

Clark loved sex. He fucking loved it.

But for all the women he'd slept with, he'd never known anyone like Melody. Maybe because she knew him, inside and out—he didn't have to withhold anything from her or pretend to be someone he wasn't. Maybe because in her own quiet way she made him feel as though everything was going to be all right. Whatever the reason, sleeping with Melody was a revelation. He didn't just make love to her. He *lost* himself in her.

"I can't believe how good it is with you," he whispered, touching his forehead to hers. "This is torture, letting you go."

"We have to let go."

She was right. He knew it. He had never been in a long-term relationship. She had enormous trust issues. No amount of good sex could alter the fact that they'd tear each other apart and destroy their friendship in the process. And Clark wouldn't be able to live with himself if that happened.

So Clark gorged himself on her, burning away the morning making love to her as slowly as he could. He took himself to the edge, denied himself orgasm again and again until his body throbbed, incandescent with lust.

Ravenous, he embedded her scent and her taste in his brain. He memorized every curve and detail of her body so that when he was an old man sitting in his rocking chair, he could close his eyes and remember what it was like to be young, in love, and alive.

She came first, clinging to him and shuddering in silence. When he came at last, his orgasm was so intense that he almost blacked out. Which was good—he hoped the numbness would keep him from facing the fact that this was the last time they'd ever make love.

Sedate, they took separate showers, checked out of the hotel and drove to Oleander without much conversation. When Clark pulled up to her trailer, Melody turned to him and gave him a smile so beautiful in its melancholy that he gripped the steering wheel to keep from breaking down or losing his temper or both.

She leaned over and kissed his cheek. "Thank you, Clark. For everything. I'm happy about the contract."

He watched her as she walked up the steps, unlocked the front door and disappeared inside.

Yeah, he thought to himself, almost sick with sadness. *Who needs a fucking heart anyway?*

* * *

Another two weeks passed.

As promised, Lucky showed up at noon with the moving van, and Clark arrived in the truck shortly thereafter. Harmony had no problem imperiously bossing around the two big cowboys as they loaded the van with all of her furniture and boxes without complaint.

By one o'clock, the van was full and the boys were hot and sweaty. Melody poured everyone a big glass of iced tea and they sat on lawn chairs in the shade of the trailer, listening to the buzz of insects in the midday heat.

"Your electricity will be on when you arrive, right?" Melody asked. "And your landline?"

"Electricity only," Harmony replied, crunching on the ice cubes in her glass. "I'm not getting a landline."

"You have the keys? And your assigned parking space in the complex?"

"It's all taken care of. Jeez. Calm down, will you?"

Melody sighed. "Just making sure. I want everything to go smoothly for you." A hot breeze blew through the eucalyptus grove in her neighbor's yard. She'd just taken a shower but her hair was already almost dry. In two hours, she'd be starting her shift at the Silver Spur.

"I'm so glad I don't have to drive to Bakersfield every day anymore," Harmony said. "That got old real fast."

"How often are you planning on coming back, Harm?" Clark asked. He'd taken off his sweaty T-shirt and hung it on the back of the chair. Melody tried not to stare, but it was impossible: all that golden-brown muscle, glistening in the sun.

Harmony shrugged. "Maybe once a month. Depends on the shifts I get at the hospital."

"Let us know if you're in town Labor Day weekend. Mom wants you both to come to the house for a barbecue. You too, Lucky."

"Only if there are illegal fireworks and free-flowing Fireball," said Harmony. She winked at Lucky, who grinned like a lovesick fool.

Melody cleared her throat. "We'll let you know," she said to Clark.

"Good." Clark took a long drink. Drops of condensation from his glass landed on his abs and gathered in the creases of his six-pack. Melody blinked and forced herself to look away.

After a little more sisterly nagging and a quick hug, Harmony hopped into her hatchback, Lucky got in the van, and together they drove off honking. As the cars faded off in the distance, Melody stood on the lawn, arms crossed, remembering what it was like to start a new adventure like the one Harmony was about to face. She herself had left for San Diego at eighteen. She never would've guessed she'd be right back here, ten years later, her own adventure fizzled out and dead.

She didn't hear Clark come up behind her. He rested his big hands on her shoulders and gently began to massage her. His touch was warm and sure. Despite the alarms in her head about his proximity, Melody relaxed. Tension drained slowly out of her body and she let her head and arms go slack.

"You did good, Mel," he said. "She may not be grateful, but I know how hard it's been on you."

That voice. God. Commanding her in the dark. Telling her his secrets. She could listen to Clark talk forever. It had been fifteen days since they'd slept together for the last time. Her dreams were still full of him—his body, his touch, and most of all, his voice.

She turned around to face him. She was wearing a tank top, cut-offs, and flip-flops. The sun burned her bare skin, as did the way Clark's eyes skittered over her body as he tried not to stare. Unspoken attraction crackled between them, dry tinder for a fire. She had to be careful. Their friendship had taken such a beating that even now, she couldn't look him in the eye.

"You hungry?" she asked. "I made a pot of rice and some chicken *adobo*. Harmony was too excited to eat, so there's plenty."

Filipino chicken stew with garlic and vinegar. Clark raised his eyebrows. "Your mom's recipe?"

She nodded.

"I guess I could suffer through that," he joked, following her inside. All the MacKinnon boys had loved her mom's home cooking.

They kept the lights off. An oscillating electric fan stirred the warm, dark air in the kitchen as they ate. For dessert, Melody cut open a ripe watermelon. The sweet red juices gathered in a pool on her plate.

"I wanted to ask you something," Clark said, wiping his mouth with a paper napkin. "Jerome's ready to launch his truck. A local news crew is going to show up tomorrow to tape a promotional spot. He wants us there with him."

"On camera?" she asked. "Why?"

"He wants to push that he's serving grass-fed beef. He's changed the name of the truck too." Clark gave her a goofy grin. "It used to be The Big Jerome. But now he's calling it Cowboy Burgers."

Melody gave a bark of laughter. "Really? That's great! I'd love to do it." She narrowed her eyes at him. "Wait. Are you…the cowboy?"

Clark shrugged. He'd hung his hat by the door. He was still distractingly shirtless. "I guess I am."

"So you're the spokesmodel? The mascot?" She paused. "Jerome's…muse?"

"Hey, it's not like that. He's a just friend." Clark gave her a crinkle-eyed smile. "Like you."

She rolled her eyes. "If that's the case, then there's definitely something shady going on between you two."

Her words hit too close to home. A quick flash of sadness touched Clark's expression. He blinked it away, stood up and cleared the dishes. Melody shook her head at herself, feeling like a fool.

Don't make jokes like that.

She followed him to the kitchen counter and turned on the water to begin washing the dishes.

Then, behind her, she felt him again.

He was standing so close her body heat reflected against his. Her hair was piled in a messy bun on top of her head; his breath washed over her exposed nape. She wanted him so badly that she became aroused at once, her body clenching up, her nipples hardening, her senses on high alert. He hadn't even touched her.

"Shady, huh?" His hot whisper burned her skin. "You and me. Is that what you think we are?"

They hadn't avoided each other. Not exactly. But they had made every effort not to be alone together, to avoid temptation and to keep their promise to each other.

But now Melody's rules dissolved under the tremendous weight of wanting him.

"I want you so bad it hurts," he whispered.

Breathless, she turned around, grabbed him and smashed her lips to his. She wrapped her arms around his shoulders and ran her hands through his thick dark hair. His mouth was cold from the watermelon. As they kissed like the universe was collapsing around them, Clark wrapped his arms around her waist and pulled her hard against him, crushing her against all his muscle and heat.

"I need you now. Right fucking now," he growled against her lips. A man on a mission, he unbuttoned her shorts and pulled them down along with her panties. He lifted her and set her on the counter, right on the ledge of the sink. Melody kept her balance as Clark's fast hands undid his buckle, unbuttoned his fly, magically produced a condom and rolled it on in the space of ten seconds.

And then his arms were around her. Holding on to his shoulders for dear life, Melody wailed as Clark surged forward, burying himself inside her in one long, violent thrust. Pleasure flooded her bloodstream like a powerful narcotic. Clark's big thumbs rubbed her nipples through the fabric of her shirt as he kissed her, his wicked tongue tangled with hers, thick and sweet and ravenous.

Melody turned to liquid around him. Still locked in his kiss, she reached down between them and began to strum her already swollen clit with her fingers. Clark grunted when he realized what she was doing and deepened their kiss. He was a big, hard man with big appetites. He thrust even deeper. A plastic tumbler fell into the sink. A couple of forks rattled and clinked onto the floor. He slid one hand up her back between her shoulder blades. The other he used to cradle her jaw, stroking her cheek with the side of his index finger. The lazy, tender movement was at complete odds with the way he was making love to her. He fucked her like a rutting bull, slamming his body into hers, his jeans down at his knees and his belt buckle thumping against the cabinet doors.

He sucked her lower lip between his teeth and bit her gently. She looked at him and the fire in his eyes seared her with their intent.

"We were made to do this," he said. "You and me. As much as we say it's wrong. It's so fucking right."

She came at once. With a gasp, she reached down and grabbed his hips with both hands, pulling him deep as she convulsed around him, melding pain with the furious waves of pleasure that crashed into her, one after another.

"Goddamn," he whispered. "That's it. Come for me, sweetheart."

He widened his stance, bent his knees and, his amazing eyes locked on hers, changed his angle so that he was fucking into her from below. She closed her eyes, savoring the sensation of him stretching her tender, aching pussy. He made love like every time was the end of the world. He made it feel like it really was.

Her hair had fallen down into a ponytail. He grabbed the end of it and pulled it down slowly until her chin was pointed up, exposing her throat. He kissed her neck and whispered hotly against her skin, "Have you ever had it this good? Tell the truth."

God, the ego he had on him. But it was deserved. "No. Never this good," she said.

"Me neither."

He kissed her again, setting the nerves in her lips on fire. Clark reached down, hooked his hand behind one of her knees and lifted her leg higher. The angle stretched her even more and increased the blazing friction between them.

Clark broke their kiss at last and thrust forward so deep she swore she could feel him in her stomach. Still holding her tightly, he froze and closed his eyes.

When he came, every muscle in his body flexed taut as he thrust home, pumping her like a beast. They were so close together she could feel the twitching of his lower abdomen as he climaxed. She could taste his skin and smell the sharp, clean tang of his come.

God, he was beautiful. As beautiful as he was kind.

Through the haze of her own madness for him, she realized something she'd suspected from the very first time they'd kissed.

She loved him.

Anguish sliced through her like a hot knife.

Eight years—that's what she'd thrown away on a man who wouldn't commit. She promised herself she'd never again date a player. Never again try to shape a man into what she thought he should be. That was a recipe for heartbreak. Right here in her kitchen, she was mixing up a big old pot of it right now.

Clark embraced her as he caught his breath. He pressed tender kisses to her neck, stroked her back and whispered to her how beautiful she was, how lovely, how sexy.

When he withdrew at last, an overwhelming sadness hit her. They'd both broken their promise.

He went to the bathroom to clean up. When he returned, she was dressed and sitting at the kitchen table, too shaken up to know how to behave. He sat next to her, reached out and put his hand on hers.

"We can handle this, Mel."

"I feel like everything is upside down." She was quiet for a long time. "Through this whole thing with my mother and my sister and my ex, you've been so amazing. So strong and caring. Coming back to Oleander has been difficult. But you made the days bearable. Not just bearable—wonderful. I missed being around you." She looked at him and rubbed the bridge of her nose. Tension was rising in her temples. "God, I don't even know what I'm saying."

"Don't be afraid. Tell me anything," he said.

She looked him in the eye. "I need you to know. I'm incapable of having a boyfriend. I can't do it again."

"Okay," he said slowly.

"I don't want a friend that I sleep with sometimes. When there's nothing better to do. You mean more to me than that."

He nodded.

"But I don't want to avoid you. Those two weeks without you—they were torturous. I was so lonely."

"So what do you want?"

"I want things to go back the way they were. Back when we were friends. Nothing more complicated than that."

"We tried. We both know we can't go back that way either." His eyes were bright with lust. "I swear to God, I think about you all the time. Hell, we just made love and I'm thinking about it again."

"I know the cure for that," she said before she could lose her nerve. She'd been thinking about this solution for days. "Go out with other women."

He sat up. "What?"

"I'm serious. It's the only way."

"Mel, I haven't been with anyone else since we first slept together. I'm not interested in anyone else. Just you."

"That feeling will pass," she said. "When you dive back into the game, you'll be your old self again. Don't worry."

"I know you're saying this to protect yourself." He looked at her with a gaze that seared her with its heat. "But don't tell me how I feel. I know what I want."

Her old boyfriend had said all the same things to her. She had to stay clearheaded. She was a mess. How could she protect him from the poison and mistrust she knew swirled inside her, just waiting to come out? "You only think you know what you want, Clark. But you'll get bored. You'll want to go out with other women. You'll begin to resent me as your girlfriend. And then we'll break up. If we get together, we'll lose our best chance at staying friends. So there's only one logical thing to do. You need to go out with other women."

"What kind of dumbass logic is that?" He stood up and kissed her hard. Her logical mind knew he was just trying to make a point, but her toes still curled against the linoleum. When he pulled away, her heart was beating hard again. He was a damn fine lover. She wished to God he could be hers forever, but she knew the universe never granted wishes like that.

"So let me get this straight—you don't trust me to be faithful." He paused. "What can I say to convince you?"

She shook her head. "Honestly, I don't know, Clark. Words are just words." She looked down at his lips, so soft and tempting. But he wasn't hers and she wasn't his and that was that. "There was a time when I thought the adventure came with a fairytale ending. Prince Charming. The kiss that broke the spell. But it was never a fairytale. It wasn't even a story. It was a game. I played it for eight years, and I lost." She sighed and glanced up at the clock. "I'm going to be late for my shift. You have to go."

Melody was about to stand up when Clark grabbed both her hands and pinned her wrists to the table. His dark eyes blazed, and the potency of his words cut through her sadness. "I don't know what that fucker did to you to make you think this way. But you and me, Mel? This isn't a game. It was never a game."

Without saying anything else, he got up, grabbed his hat by the door and left. The screen door shut with a bang.

* * *

After dinner, Clark accompanied his eldest brother Dean out to the stables. A couple of their father's cattle dogs followed at their heels, panting and wagging in the warm August night.

"So you're taking Mr. Singh out tomorrow morning? Has he gone riding before?" Clark asked. He turned on the lights.

"Once or twice, he said." Dean led out D.B. Cooper, a big buckskin quarter horse that was ten years old and bombproof. Nothing spooked him. "I think old boy here will do just fine for *Papa ji,* won'tcha, D.B.?"

Clark smiled. His brother had more to say to livestock than he ever had to say to people. "You want to ride mine?"

"Yeah, sure."

Clark got Joker's halter on and led him out of his stall. A four-year-old bay roan gelding, Joker was one of the best working horses Clark had ever owned.

They set to work, using rubber currycombs and dandy brushes to remove all the dirt and dust from the horses' coats. While Clark took a hoof pick to their feet, Dean finished their coats with a thorough brushing and ran a soft brush over their faces. Dean and Clark had been doing this since they were boys. It was easy to fall into a rhythm as they worked.

"So, how are things going with Monica's family?" Clark asked. He couldn't face his own worries right now. It was easier to focus on Dean's. "Have you won them over yet?"

Dean snorted. "Me? I'm scratching the surface yet. Her mom seems to like me. Her dad, eh." Dean waved his palm back and forth. "Her brother wants to see my head on a pike."

Clark knew his stubborn big brother was wildly in love with a woman whose family didn't approve of him. So Dean did what he did best—he took the bull by the horns and didn't back down. He'd taken it upon himself to woo them all, come hell or high water. And Clark was certain that the crazy bastard could do it.

"I have to tell you something," Clark said, "and you can't tell anyone else about it."

"Aw, hell, what now?"

"Promise."

"What are we, seven?" When Clark frowned at him, Dean said, "All right, for Chrissakes. I promise."

Clark took a deep breath and cleared his throat. "So, um. Melody and me…we've been fooling around."

Dean stopped brushing Joker's face. "Did I hear you right? Did you just say *Melody*?"

The MacKinnon boys had grown up with the Santos girls. Clark's confession was on par with admitting incest. "I know, I know," Clark said quickly. "It's a less-than-ideal situation."

"Dad's gonna gut you, you know that, right?" Dean's words were scary and probably true, but he was smiling. "Damn, Clark. That's a doozy."

"Tell me about it. But here's the thing, Dean. She's not just another girl. Not to me."

Clark told the whole story, soup to nuts. Of course, he left out how good Melody was in bed. On balcony. In kitchen.

"I don't know what to do next." Clark led Joker back into the stall and gave him some oats. "She's spooked, but I don't want us to stay here, in limbo. She deserves more—much more."

Dean gathered up all their tools and put up D.B. for the night. "So, let me get this straight. You can't just be friends."

"Right."

"You can't be boyfriend and girlfriend."

"Right."

"You can't be each other's booty call."

Clark nodded. "You've got the measure of it."

"Hmm." Dean sat down on an upturned bucket and petted the dogs. He said nothing for a long time. Joker nickered in the quiet, enjoying his oats. Clark looked out into the dark farmyard, the corrals, and the pastures beyond. Across those hills and down the highway was

Melody's house. He wondered if she was thinking of him.

"Do you love her?" Dean's voice startled him out of his daydreaming.

The answer was so easy, it surprised him. "Yeah. I do." Clark turned around. "I don't want to lose her."

One of the dogs rested his head on Dean's knee. "I could tell you what I'd do," Dean said, "but you might not have the stomach for it."

Clark snorted. "You're a professional bullfighter. You referee bucking bulls in rodeo arenas. Nobody has your stomach."

"Maybe so." Dean scratched the scruff of the dog's neck. "But the truth is, the best thing you can do with something that scares you is face it. Head-on."

"How do I do that?"

Dean looked up and grinned. "Let's go see if Mom's still awake."

* * *

Jerome's bright-orange lunch truck sparkled in the Santa Monica sunshine. The words *Cowboy Burgers* were emblazoned on the side of the truck in white letters alongside a logo: a cowboy on a bucking bronco, a big hamburger in his free hand. The truck was camera ready. The bustling farmers' market served as a colorful backdrop. Its stands were crammed with a rainbow of summer produce—tomatoes, corn, kale, blueberries, peaches. A small crowd of curious onlookers and market regulars gathered around the truck.

Clark had brought Jerome one of his cowboy hats to wear for the TV segment. It was black, not surprisingly. Jerome wore his black chef's jacket, black jeans and black sneakers.

"Hey, Johnny Cash. You ready for your close-up?" Clark asked.

"You know it, bro!" Jerome said with a smile, tipping his hat.

Melody thought it was odd that Clark had made such an effort to dress nicely himself. Clean-shaven, he was wearing new jeans and a freshly pressed blue plaid shirt that he'd kept hung up in the van during the drive. With his white Resistol straw hat and polished belt buckle, he looked every bit the hot cowboy Hollywood dreams were made of.

Melody stood by the truck as the camera crew set up. Feeling like an extra on the set, Melody wore a cobalt-blue sundress her sister had left in the closet. She'd polished her cowboy boots and did her best to make her hair and makeup look halfway decent.

"Nice duds, Clark!"

Melody's old friend the yoga goddess stalked up to Clark. In sweatpants, a bikini top and aviator sunglasses, the blonde looked like an ad for coconut water in a surfing magazine. She and Clark chatted quietly out of Melody's earshot as Melody stared blankly at the sodas and bottled water lined up like soldiers in the lunch truck's cooler.

Don't be angry. He can talk to anyone he wants, she told herself in silence. *You told him to see other women, remember?*

Melody gritted her teeth, unable to stand the taste of her own bad medicine.

When she looked up, the yoga goddess was gone. Jerome and Clark were talking to the TV reporter, a chubby gentleman in a shirt and tie. The sound guy and the cameraman gave the thumbs-up and it was time to begin.

Melody stood up straight and tried to relax her shoulders so she wouldn't look like a spazz on camera. It was a live segment. Back home, the entire town was watching. Tom Shelton told her that he would put the show on in the bar.

Clark leaned over and whispered in her ear, "You look so fucking beautiful."

She didn't have time to respond.

Three, two, one. Showtime.

The reporter gave a quick rundown of Jerome's impressive career then asked him questions about his inspiration and his menu for the food truck. Jerome, in his element, was chatty and cheerful. One of his cooks handed hot food out of the window of the truck and the reporter taste-tested everything with glowing praise.

"Now, I see that you have a couple of friends here with you. The name of your truck is Cowboy Burgers. How did you arrive at that name?" asked the reporter.

"Some people think California is all about surfers and movie stars," said Jerome. "But I would come every Wednesday to this market and I met this guy right here. He's a real California cowboy. He's the inspiration for my truck."

"And what's your name?"

"Clark MacKinnon, sir. This is Melody Santos. We're from MacKinnon Ranch, a family-owned and -operated cattle ranch located in Oleander, California. We produce 100 percent pasture-raised grass-fed beef, no hormones."

Like a pro, Clark went into all of the benefits of grass-fed beef, including better taste and better nutrition. "We're a small operation, not a factory farm. Our animals wander the pastures, get lots of exercise and fresh air. They've never seen a feedlot. In truth, my parents, my brothers and I—we're in the business of raising good grass. If you do that, the cows will do the rest."

Jerome chimed in. "By the way, I know what your audience is thinking. He doesn't mean that kind of grass, okay, guys?"

Melody covered her smile. Clark's eyes darted to hers before he turned back to the reporter. "With Jerome's help, we're hoping to spread the word about our operation and our products. God willing, my family will be able to do this work for years to come." He cleared his throat. A bright red flush crept up his neck. "Actually, Stan, I was hoping Melody could help me with something important with regards to that."

The reporter looked fazed for a moment. "Uh, sure. What do you have in mind?"

Melody's eyes widened. She kept the smile plastered on her face despite every alarm going off in her head. Live television! Thousands of people watching! What was this crazy cowboy up to?

With a nod at Jerome, Clark took off his hat and pulled something from his shirt pocket.

When he got down on one knee, the crowd gasped. A couple of women suppressed squeals.

Melody froze.

Sweet. Baby. Jesus.

If Elvis Presley had come swooping down on the back of a solid-gold pterodactyl, Melody would not have been more shocked. With an expression of expectant glee, the reporter lowered the microphone to Clark's mouth.

"Melody Santos," Clark said slowly, looking up at her, "you're beautiful, strong, and courageous. I've never known you to run from challenges. You're my partner in crime and the best friend I could ever ask for. You said you were looking for your fairytale ending. Well, I can't give you that. What I can give you is the rest of my story. I want us to write it together. I want it to be our story." He licked his lips. He was red as a tomato. "You and me, what we are now—that happened real fast. But when I know something, I know it." With a nervous smile, he gestured to the camera and the crowd. "And I want the whole world to know it too." He took her hand and stroked her fingers. "I love you. Will you marry me?"

Melody stared blankly at him, her brain struggling to process what was happening.

Who did this kind of thing?

Who jumped from friend to one-night stand to engaged like some kind of deranged bullfrog?

The Clark she thought she knew was a player and a flirt. He didn't believe in long-term relationships. He'd never had a girlfriend.

But the Clark kneeling in front of her today was telling the world a different story. He loved her. He wanted to be her husband. He was making a promise to her even though there were no guarantees that she wouldn't break his heart in front of thousands of people. The naked vulnerability in his expression made her chest ache.

He was right. This was no game.

There was crazy and then there was Clark MacKinnon crazy—her kind of crazy. And only one answer blazed in front of her, crystal clear.

"Yes," she said. "Yes, I'll marry you."

He put his hat back on and slipped the ring on her finger. Before she had a chance to look at it, her big cowboy grabbed her and swung her around in a circle. The crowd cheered as the elated reporter signed off on the segment, sniffling and a little teary-eyed.

When the cameras were off, Clark put her down and leaned in for the kiss.

"You okay?" he said.

"No," she whispered. As she stroked his cheek, her pretty diamond ring glittered in the sunlight. "Where did you get this?"

"It was my grandmother's. I asked my mom for it last night." He grinned. "She cried for an hour."

"If my son were marrying a girl like me, I'd cry for an hour too."

They looked at each other, smiling like idiots.

"I love you, Clark," she said.

Clark nodded. "Yeah. I know."

"Even though you're a little screwed in the head."

"So are you, sweetheart. We make a good match." He dipped his head but she dodged the kiss.

"Wait. Promise me one more thing," she said, putting her fingertip to his lips.

He lifted an eyebrow. "Something tells me this is not going to be the last thing."

"Hush. Promise me you won't do that thing anymore—that eye thing you do when you're picking up women. The one where you memorize their eye color."

"What eye thing? You mean this?"

When Clark looked into her eyes, warmth suffused Melody's body and all of the clatter and racket of the world fell quiet. In the shelter of that beautiful, dark gaze, Melody learned the truth. She held his attention not because she was the most beautiful or fascinating woman in the world, but because he had chosen to give it to her, along with his promise of a lifetime of love. Marrying Clark seemed like an insane gamble. But in her heart she knew it was a safe one.

"Kiss me," she whispered.

Her best friend took her in his arms and smiled. "With pleasure."

Who needs luck when you can get Lucky?

Please see the next page for a preview of

Cowboy Karma

*Sometimes the thing you throw away
becomes the thing you most desire.*

—GABRIELLE HAMILTON

HARMONY SANTOS PUT DOWN her fork with a clink. "Wait a second. Are you breaking up with me? On my birthday?"

Dr. Franklin Walker Vallejo Lockwood had so many names, she couldn't keep track of them. He was Dr. Lockwood to their patients at Bakersfield General Hospital. To the other surgical nurses in their ward, he was Dr. Dreamboat. To his wealthy, doting parents, he was Franklin, beloved only child. To Harmony, he was simply Frank, her boyfriend of almost a year.

In the candlelight, Frank looked up at her with those bright green eyes and said, "I don't think this is working out, Harm."

"What do you mean?" She was genuinely confused. "We're working out great."

"Just hear me out."

He had prepared a list of vague reasons, but Harmony was too tied up in her shock to understand anything coming out of his mouth.

This wasn't supposed to happen.

When Dr. Dreamboat finally asked her out after she'd crushed on him for months, Harmony believed her love life had come to a happy crescendo. Cue rainbows. Puppies. Blue skies. They'd been together almost a year. In good time, Harmony Santos, R.N. was certain she'd become Mrs. Harmony Santos-Lockwood, wife of the crown prince of Bakersfield.

This was no daydream. Over the last year, she'd worked her ass off to become the kind of woman worthy of this relationship. Taking her cues from Frank, she'd stopped partying and raising Cain. She learned to curb her impulsive temper, something that often got her in trouble when she was younger. Frank had complimented her on her improvements. These days, far as Harmony could see, they were the perfect couple. Doctor and nurse. Proper prince and princess. Happily ever after, forever and ever.

But now?

Still unable to grasp the meaning of his words, Harmony watched his face as he spoke. He looked sorry—the quintessential sorry person, sweet and sincere. Dr. Dreamboat did even awkward things like dumping his girlfriend on her birthday appear easy.

Rage. Confusion. Hurt. Heartache. Too many emotions to keep bottled up at once—Harmony panicked. She had to get the hell out of here.

While he was in midsentence, she stood up, opened her purse, and dropped some money on the table.

"Baby, don't do that." Frank glanced down at the bills and back up at her. "Where are you going?"

"Home. I'm going home." Keeping her face still, Harmony turned and walked out of the fancy restaurant.

Trembling, she called her older sister from the highway. Melody picked up right away. "Hey, birthday girl. What's up?"

The words came out on their own. "I'm coming down."

"Why? What's wrong?"

Tears welled in Harmony's eyes, but she forced herself not to cry. *No blubbering.* She made her voice hard and clear. "Frank—he dumped me. Tonight."

"Oh, crap." Melody fell quiet. Harmony heard the muffled voice of her brother-in-law asking a question. "My sister's boyfriend just broke up with her. Yeah. On her birthday." Melody turned back to the phone. "Listen, we're not at home right now."

"What?" Now panic swirled inside her along with all those other messy emotions. Harmony didn't trust herself tonight, alone in her apartment with her freshly broken heart. "Where are you guys?"

"We're driving to the Silver Spur."

"The Spur?" Harmony sniffed. "Tonight? Why?"

"Tonight's the grand reopening. Come meet us there."

Someone grabbed the phone. "Harm? This is Clark. Forget that prick and get your cowgirl ass to Oleander." A series of deep whoops and hollers sounded in the background. His brothers and their girls were with him—instant party.

Harmony blinked. Noise, drinking, dancing, and her crazy patched-together family—she hadn't been out in ages. This sounded like just the ticket out of Shitsville. "All right," she said. "I'm coming."

Melody got back on the line. "See you soon, girl."

* * *

One-and-a-half hours later, her jumbled-up feelings in check, Harmony climbed out of her Jeep into a parking lot jam-packed with pickup trucks. She took a deep breath—warm summer air, sagebrush, and cow funk. The smell of Oleander. The smell of home.

She gave herself a once-over—black mini-dress from her date, beat-up cowboy boots she'd had in the car—and made a beeline for the crowd of people standing outside the Silver Spur, the newly remodeled cowboy bar where she had spent many an hour of her degenerate youth.

But *this*—this wasn't the rundown honky-tonk she remembered.

This was a gleaming, two-story cowboy palace. Its log-cabin exterior was lit up with strings of white lights and planted out with drought-resistant landscaping. Harmony stood gawking at the joint until her sister texted her.

I'm standing by the bouncer.

Melody wore Daisy Dukes, a glittery tank top, and brand-new cowboy boots. Her hair was curled and eyeliner accentuated her beautiful brown eyes. When Harmony hugged her big sister, an enormous wave of relief washed over her. She was home—and she might be able to salvage this horrible night.

"Look at you, gorgeous." Harmony squinted at Melody. "Hey, what's that?" She lifted her sister's hair off her neck. There was a small purple mark just beneath her earlobe.

Melody flipped her hair back to cover the hickey. "It's nothing."

Harmony rolled her eyes. "Can't that boy keep his hands off you?"

"Not really. Come on."

A big bouncer removed the velvet rope from the entrance and let them cut in front of the line. As soon as she saw the scene inside the new Silver Spur, Harmony knew she was right to leave Bakersfield behind tonight.

The original Silver Spur had been a stalwart but rather nasty piece of Oleander's history, a place for beer bottles, fists, and ugly faces to get acquainted. When Harmony first snuck into the Spur, she was seventeen years old. That was seven years ago. The only decorations in the place had been dusty beer signs and a distinguished group of grizzled locals.

But this—this was nothing like the old Spur. Owner Tom Shelton had built a flashy country-western nightclub. A long bar lined the back wall, manned by an army of sexy bartenders in cowboy hats slinging up beers and shots. A stone wall and a big fireplace lined another wall. Around the enormous sunken dance floor was a brass rail where patrons could lean, chat, and check out everyone else's dance moves. Doors led to vast smoking patios. And up front, under what looked like a mirrored disco saddle, was a big stage bathed in purple light and covered with dancers. A DJ stood in the booth on the edge of the dance floor, spinning boot-scootin' country music to the enthusiastic crowd.

"Holy moly, Mel," Harmony said. "Tom did this?"

Melody stood close enough to speak directly into Harmony's ear over the sound of the music. "He knocked the old place down and rebuilt it from the ground up. He's got musical acts booked up almost two years in advance. Big names too. He knows a lot of promoters.

We're going to have tons of bands coming through here. It'll be a blast."

"I can't believe it." She looked up at the big, ornate chandeliers made of antlers. "Where will I throw up at the end of the night?

Her sister snorted. "Not in here. Tom will blacklist you."

"We could throw up anywhere we wanted in the old place."

"It's a new day, Harm."

She followed her sister to a large, circular banquette just to the left of the stage. Some familiar faces sat in the shadows, drinking beer and talking—Melody's in-laws, the MacKinnons, old family friends. Melody's husband Clark sat on the end. Melody went to him right away and sat in his lap. They were so damn cute that Harmony wanted to throw up a little—in her mouth, so she wouldn't get in trouble with Tom.

"Happy birthday, stranger," Clark said. "Glad you came out."

Harmony bent and kissed her handsome brother-in-law on the cheek. "Hey, doofus."

"We'll kick his ass for you. Just say the word."

"I'll keep that in mind." She said hello to the other two folks at the table, Clark's brother Daniel MacKinnon and his wife Georgia, on a rare night out from their four kids.

Georgia was wearing a red dress. Daniel couldn't keep his eyes off her.

"Too much lovey-dovey in this booth," Harmony whispered to her sister. "I'm going to get a drink. You want anything?"

Melody shook her head as Clark leaned forward and kissed her neck.

Harmony walked through the crowd. The room was steamy with dancing and pheromones. She ordered a Bud Light and ran the icy bottle over her forehead.

As she stood at the brass rail and checked out the dancers, she recognized a handful of childhood friends and old nursing-school classmates in the arms of their boyfriends or boyfriends-for-the-night. Old-timers took their turns on the dance floor, the smoothest dancers of all. Near the front of the stage, she spotted Dean, the eldest MacKinnon brother, dancing sexy with his wife Monica. They looked unspeakably happy. Everyone did. With a grimace, Harmony killed her beer and left the bottle on a nearby tray.

A sense of misery crept over her, clinging to her like a big, wet monkey. She hated that Frank had hurt her. But even worse, she hated that she'd allowed herself to be vulnerable enough for him to do that. After months of pining followed by months of self-improvement, she'd finally gotten the man she wanted.

Trouble was, he didn't want her.

Harmony winced. *Goddammit. This pain.*

A new song started up. Shaking off her melancholy, she strode right into the heart of the crowded dance floor. Steve Earle's "Copperhead Road"—an easy line dance. She counted her way in and soon was stomping across the dance floor. The loud music pounded in her chest. Even though it had been years since she'd line danced, her body knew the steps without her thinking about them. The heartache receded a little.

More dancing. Maybe some shots. Maybe making out with a stranger. That'll keep me from feeling...this. Whatever this ugly feeling is.

She danced solo for three more songs. Then an old-timer led her in a waltz. The country gentleman was followed by a baby-faced cowboy in a camo baseball cap. She danced three more songs with him and bid him goodbye with a hug and a kiss on the cheek—too young.

The DJ took the mike. "Next up, the cowboy cha-cha."

A slower dance. Harmony fanned herself with her hand and thought this might be a good time to grab a shot of Fireball chased with another beer.

She turned to leave the dance floor when a big warm hand rested on her shoulder.

"Wait. Don't go yet."

She turned. In the dark, the new cowboy's face was obscured in the shadow of his hat. The DJ cued up an old Bellamy Brothers song Harmony remembered her father loved. It began, "If I said you had a beautiful body would you hold it against me?" She knew the words as surely as she knew her own name.

The dancers around them paired off in a hurry and got into the sweetheart position. Everyone counted off together and started around the massive dance floor in a counter-clockwise direction, all in time.

Before Harmony could say anything, the stranger took her hands and spun her. His movements were sure and strong. He was an experienced dancer, not someone who had to be babysat around the floor.

"Been a long time, hasn't it?" he said.

She stole sideways glances at him. Tall and muscular, he wore a black hat and a plaid shirt with the sleeves rolled up. His forearms were thick and smooth. She could see that he had a strong jaw, a dark, short beard, and dark skin. He spoke crystal-clear English with a Mexican accent.

"You don't remember me, do you, Harmony?"

She stared.

A half-smile. "Guess I'm just another cowboy to you."

For strangers, they moved in perfect rhythm. Harmony felt grateful that he was a strong lead since her brain was otherwise occupied with trying to figure out who he was. When he brought their bodies together, chest to chest, she looked up at him. His body gave off controlled strength and a smooth, unnerving calm. At last, she peeked under the shadow of his cowboy hat.

Dark brows. Bedroom eyes the color of whiskey.

No way. "Lucky?"

Lucero "Lucky" Garcia had gone to Harmony's high school and worked as a ranch hand for the MacKinnons. She'd always known who he was, but they were never friends. Two years ago, before Harmony had left for Bakersfield, she and Lucky shared one freaky, drunken make-out session at her graduation party. For days afterward, Lucky followed her around like a puppy. After he'd helped her move to her new apartment, she'd given him a kiss on the cheek and promised to call him. But fate had different plans. That Monday, she started working at the hospital. Dr. Dreamboat entered her romantic crosshairs and she immediately forgot the existence of other men.

The Lucky of her memory was a boyish flyweight. At the time, he was still living at home with his mom. Sweet as candy, he was enthusiastic and optimistic. Everything about him screamed inexperience, sexual and otherwise.

Disoriented, Harmony stared up at her partner. The Lucky of her memory was nothing like the Lucky who held her in his arms tonight. His movements were sure as he led her around the dance floor, anticipating her every step. And he'd put on lots of muscle. His broad arms and shoulders strained against his shirt, and when he turned, she saw that his back narrowed into a tight V in Wranglers wrapped around a sexy, meaty ass. Harmony tried not to stare. Lucky had been working out. The effects were downright breathtaking.

"You look surprised to see me."

"The MacKinnons didn't tell me you were here," she said.

"No one knows I'm here. I just got back this afternoon."

"Back from what?"

"I've been on the road."

"Doing what?"

He smiled. His lips were sensual and full, pretty and manly at the same time. Dr. Dreamboat was handsome, but he had thin lips. Kissing him sometimes felt like making out with a mail slot.

"So you really don't remember me," Lucky said softly.

The man was sexy. And annoying. "Of course I remember you." She fluttered her eyelashes like a cartoon princess. "How could I forget? I've been watching your career, tracking your every move, wishing on a star that one day we'd meet again."

Lucky grinned. "There she is. There's the sassy Harmony I remember." He spun her again, hard. Her hair whipped around. God help her, he was a good dancer. Had they danced when they'd gotten together two years ago? She would've remembered this.

He pulled her close, his hand on her waist sure and steady. Their thighs touched, his hard, muscular one thick between her legs as they swayed. He looked down at her. The heat in his eyes surprised her. She pressed her lips together and turned away, his gaze too intense for her to meet up close.

"You never called me," he said. "Were you just using me?"

Seamlessly, the DJ faded out the Bellamy Brothers and cued up "Neon Moon" by Brooks and Dunn. The dancers on the floor altered their rhythm. Lucky picked it up without a hitch.

"You didn't like being used?" she asked.

"To be honest, I would've liked being used more. Harder." The sexy bastard grinned.

The slow song turned their movements even more liquid, more sensual. As she and Lucky made their way through the crowd, she put everything else out of her mind—the couples dancing close to them, the sharp scent of fresh paint and strong whiskey, the hungry ache rising inside her. In anticipation of her birthday date with Dr. Dreamboat, she'd laid off using her vibrator all week. Her body was primed and aching for sex. Lucky pulled her even closer against him. He smelled good. Fabric softener. Musk. Spice. His whole body was hard underneath his clothes. She struggled to keep her arousal under wraps, but he was making it extremely difficult.

"How about you, Harmony?" Her name on his lips was like a magic spell. "Do you like to be used?"

She closed her eyes. *Why does he feel so damn good?* "Sometimes."

He lowered his lips to her ear. "How about tonight? Do you want to be used tonight?"

She shivered. She would like nothing more than to lose herself tonight. She could feel the pain stalking her like a wolf in the dark, and she wanted to be numb before it got her. Numb with anything—drinking, dancing, sex. Anything to protect herself from the howling pain she knew was coming. She locked her hands behind his neck. "Dance with me. Dance with me the rest of the night."

"Then?"

"Then we'll see, cowboy."

Feisty reporter vs. gruff cowboy—
buckle up for a hard ride.

Please see the next page for a preview of

Cowboy Rising

Curiosity is the lust of the mind.

—THOMAS HOBBES

AT THE END OF A LONG DAY riding and talking beef with Clark, Georgia drove to the dilapidated Rambling Ranch Inn, checked in, showered, and lay sleepless on the musty bed. The Oleander livestock auction was happening tomorrow morning. She'd be able to make a lot of contacts there, but she needed a good night's rest. Usually a little mindless T.V. was all it took to put her to sleep. But tonight was different.

Something about that jerk Daniel MacKinnon had gotten under her skin. She was antsy even though she should've been tired. She was feverish even though her room was cold.

Restlessness—she'd battled that feeling all her life. She knew herself. There was only one solution. She needed to get out.

After changing into a fresh pair of jeans and a white camisole, Georgia threw on her beat-up leather jacket and boots. She applied a quick coat of mascara and a little lipstick, jumped into her car, and drove into town. *This is the ticket.* She smiled to herself. A beer. A game of pool. A little flirting. Something—anything—to take this edge off.

A half-dozen dusty pickup trucks and a couple of motorcycles were parked in front of the Silver Spur, the old dive bar she'd spotted from the highway on her drive into town. The crisp night air nipped at her cheeks as she walked from her car to the entrance. A heavyset cowboy in a fancy embroidered shirt checked her ID and waved her in through the plain wooden door.

"Have a good time, Miss Meyers," he said.

She replied, "I aim to."

Tanya Tucker's "A Little Too Late" blared on the jukebox. Half-busted neon beer signs illuminated the dank wood-paneled room and the smell of stale beer, mildew, and old leather hit her nose. A lone string of Christmas lights hung above the cash register next to a grungy plastic statue of Santa Claus. In a lifetime of crisscrossing the country, Georgia had been in a hundred honky-tonks just like this one. She could've been anywhere. The Silver Spur happened to be in Oleander, California.

After quickly sizing up the crowd, she took a seat at the bar in a gap between a group of bikers and a group of old cowboys. The grizzled woman behind the bar greeted her with a grunt and set a pint of beer in front of her. Georgia took a sip. It was cold. That's all it needed to be.

"You enjoying that Colorado Kool-Aid?" One of the cowboys turned to her and tipped his hat. He wasn't as old as the rest. His mustache gone salt-and-pepper, but his dark face was handsome and his eyes were kind. "Herman Hernandez. Call me Manny. Nice to meet you."

Manny introduced her to the rest of his friends, all benevolent old-timers with ready smiles and twinkles in their eyes. The longer she chatted with them, the more Georgia realized she missed her dad—she hadn't seen him since his Air Force retirement party a few years ago. These days he lived in Montana with his fourth wife and her teenaged kids. As much as she'd enjoy visiting him, Georgia didn't want to impose on his new family.

More patrons shoehorned themselves into the Silver Spur as the night wore on. The old men were entertaining her with funny stories when on the other side of the room, a beer glass shattered on the floor and a sudden silence descended on the crowd. Tension rose and crackled in the air like electricity. Georgia turned around to see what was going on.

A couple motorcycle dudes stood by the pool table facing down a cowboy swaying on his feet.

"Try it," said the cowboy in a deep, raspy voice. "I dare you."

Manny lowered his voice. "Stupid kid's got a death wish."

The female bartender shook her head. "Can you blame him, Manny? With what he's been through lately?"

Georgia squinted in the darkness. *Wait a second. Is that Daniel?*

The bouncer in his embroidered shirt shouldered his way in, stood in between the bikers and the cowboy, and escorted the cowboy outside. "You're done, MacKinnon," said the big man. "Let's go."

Georgia reached into her purse, dropped a few bills on the bar, and bade the old-timers a quick goodbye. She rushed outside. Her eyes couldn't believe what they saw—stuck-up Daniel MacKinnon, brought low by something as pedestrian as whiskey and an insult. Drunk as a skunk, he wore a white hat, jeans, and a pressed plaid shirt with a beer spilled down the front of it. The bouncer leaned him up against the side of the bar and gave him a talking-to.

"Two nights in a row. This isn't like you. You're hurting, Dan. You want me to call someone to come pick you up?"

"No—don't. Don't call anyone."

"You can't stay here."

"Just a little longer. I'll be all right. I don't need a ride."

"You need to sleep it off. You need a bed." The bouncer took out his cell phone. "I'm calling Clark."

Daniel shook his head. Even in his drunkenness, he looked panicked. "Wait—"

Georgia stepped forward. "My car's here. I can take him home."

Both men looked up, noticing her for the first time. To her surprise, Daniel reached forward and rested his arm on her shoulders. Unsteady on his feet, he used her like a crutch, leaning his considerable weight on her. "Yup. That'll do," he slurred. "She'll take me home."

The bouncer raised his eyebrows and put his phone back in his pocket. "Do you two know each other?"

"Me'n her? Good buddies," said Daniel. "Ain't we, Scoop?"

She nodded, fascination and disgust mixing together in her tummy. "Yup. Real good."

Daniel's big hand gripped her shoulder as she turned and walked him to the car. She unlocked the door, threw her books and papers into the back seat, and shoved six feet of drunken cowboy into her little hatchback. As she leaned over him to clip his seatbelt in place, Daniel looked up at her. "You are probably well aware of this," he drawled, "but you are pretty as *fuck*."

In the dark and cold, Georgia felt the boozy heat rising off his skin. "Well, aren't you a silver-tongued devil."

His glassy eyes latched onto hers. "A silver tongue can't do what mine can, Miss Meyers."

Even though her lady parts clenched up hungrily inside her at his words, Georgia couldn't let any man get away with a comment like that. She stood up straight. "Do what? You mean *offend* me? You're right about that, Mr. MacKinnon." She slammed the door on his handsome, smirking face and walked around the hood.

As she started up the engine, Georgia wondered how the night had taken such an odd turn. As usual, she embraced the weirdness. "Tell me," she said, pulling onto the empty highway, "why'd you foist me on your brother for the day? You're clearly the one who knows what's going on."

"Aw, come on now. Clark's all right. Didn't he tell you everything you needed to know?"

Georgia conceded that point. "He did. But I had to lead him around to get him to say the right stuff. He's still a kid."

"True. Unfortunately."

She turned his cryptic statement over in her mind. *What does he mean by "unfortunately"?* "Your dad—he seemed eager to talk to me when I contacted him earlier this week. What happened? Why wasn't he on the ranch today?"

Daniel fiddled with the vents of her heater and ignored her question. "What year is this dinosaur?"

Georgia blew out an annoyed breath. "1985."

"No shit?" He played with the knobs of her busted radio. "Does it come with a flux capacitor?" When she didn't react, he said, "Haven't you seen *Back to the Future?*"

"I know what a flux capacitor is, you dork," she said testily. "Don't make fun of my ride. It's my car. I bought it. I take care of it."

"So I take it the newspaper business ain't doing so well?"

"It's doing about as good as the cattle business. Only I don't have to shove my arms up a cow's see-you-next-Tuesday just to make a living."

"You have a point there. But you rake as much shit as I do. Probably more." He grinned at her and tipped forward drunkenly before the seatbelt caught. "Aw, what's wrong, Scoop? You dish it out but you can't take it, can you?"

"You better be sober enough to walk once we get to the ranch," she seethed, "'cuz I'm dumping your ass on the driveway and leaving you there."

He raised his head. "No. I can't go to the ranch."

"What? Why not?"

Daniel swallowed hard. "You gotta take me somewhere else."

"Podunk town at midnight? Where the hell do you want me to take you?" She frowned. "What's wrong with the ranch?"

He made a fist and tapped it softly on his knee. "Nothing's wrong with the ranch, it's just…" He trailed off.

"What?"

He fell quiet long enough that she looked over at him. In the dashboard lights, the saddened expression on his face made her heart unexpectedly stutter in her chest. The stuck-up prick she'd met this morning was completely gone. In his place sat a man—a young man, but a man nonetheless—who carried a heavy burden. She couldn't see what it was, but she could feel it, dragging him down like a stone.

"What's wrong?" she asked.

"My younger brothers," he said. "Clark and Caleb. They can't—they can't see me like this."

Christ. Georgia gripped her steering wheel tighter. In silence, she drove on, passing the turnoff to MacKinnon Ranch and hurtling into the darkness as if the answer to their problem lay somewhere out there in the desert.

"Any other family I could take you to?" she asked.

He shook his head.

"Friends?" She paused. "Girlfriend?"

"No. There's nobody."

She drove a few more minutes. She had a solution, but she needed a moment to come to terms with what she was about to do. *You went out looking for excitement, Gigi. You sure found it.*

"All right," she said at last. "I know where to go."

She slowed down, pulled a Y-turn in the soft dirt, and headed for the Rambling Ranch Inn.

* * *

Georgia bought two cups of coffee from the vintage vending machine that stood forlorn in the front office. The night clerk, a sour-looking old man in a Coors T-shirt with cut-off sleeves, peered over the high counter and gave her the stink-eye. She gave it right back.

When she returned to the room, Daniel sat on the bed facing away from her. He'd stripped off his beer-soaked shirt and removed his hat. His white cotton undershirt stretched across his broad shoulders, highlighting the sharp V of his back. Her brain automatically compared Daniel to his brother. Even though Clark was meatier, the leanness and balanced proportions of Daniel's body made Georgia's mouth water.

She put the coffee down on the nightstand. "I doubt sugar or cream will improve this."

Daniel turned and looked at her over his shoulder. The lamplight made his green eyes feral. "Thanks."

She took off her leather jacket. A thrill ran through her as his gaze took a slow ride up and down her body. She sat down at the table and took a tentative sip of mud. "You're looking a little better."

"Getting there." He ran a big hand through his short hair, mussing it slightly, then leaned back on his arms. The caps of muscle on his shoulders bulged, as did the muscles in his thighs as he stretched out his long legs. "So. Georgia Meyers. You ask questions for a living."

"Sure do."

"Let's switch. Tell me your story. Where are you from?"

She gave him her usual canned line. "Everywhere and nowhere."

He frowned. "What does that mean?"

"I was born in Germany. Air Force base. Moved around a lot as a kid." When he didn't say anything, she added, "My mom's family's from Oklahoma. My grandmother had a ranch there. Sheep, mostly."

"Is that where you learned to ride horses?"

She nodded.

He took a sip of coffee, made a face, and put the cup back down on the nightstand. "I'm guessing that was...a while ago?"

She cracked a smile. "Hey, at least I didn't fall off."

Daniel MacKinnon was not impressed. "You'll be sore tomorrow. Take some aspirin."

Georgia didn't want to admit she was hurting right now, or that the hungry ache inside her had nothing to do with saddles. "What else do you want to know about me?"

"You got a boyfriend?"

His direct approach was refreshing. Too many people circled around what they meant. He wasn't one of them. "I had a boyfriend back in Raleigh. We broke up when I moved to Fresno."

"How long ago was that?"

"About two years."

"That's a long time without a man."

She raised an eyebrow at him. "It's been a long time since I've had a *boyfriend*, not a man. Big difference, kid."

He said nothing for a moment, staring at her with a cool, unbroken gaze. "I'm not a kid," he said at last.

"How old are you?"

"Twenty-four."

"You're a kid to me."

He leaned forward. Lamplight caught the golden hair on his thick forearms. "So what's wrong with having a boyfriend? A husband? That not your thing? Are you one of them feminists?"

That got her hackles up. "Here's a newsflash for you. Lots of women are feminists whether they admit it to big dumb Okies like you or not."

"All right. Here's a newsflash for *you*, Scoop." He smirked. "My people are from Missouri and Ohio. There's only one big dumb Okie in this room and I ain't it."

Georgia smiled. He was fun to talk to, at least. She remembered something his brother had said. "You just graduated, didn't you?"

He nodded.

"What did you study?"

He shrugged. "Nothing I can use now."

"Tell me."

"You wouldn't believe me. I'm just a big dumb Okie in your eyes."

"Try me."

"Wish I could 'try you,' Miss Meyers," he said, "but I don't have one-night stands with feminists. As a rule."

She *tsk*ed. "That's a shame."

"How so?"

"We usually do the things the other girls don't do."

He lowered his voice and narrowed his eyes. "Like what?"

"Guess you'll never know, will you?"

When Daniel pursed his lips and released them, goose bumps rose on Georgia's skin. Silence filled the room, thickening the air with tension. When he flexed his jaw, a muscle shifted in his temple. Up close, his dirty blond hair was more golden than brown. She wanted to touch it. She wanted to run her fingers through it while he kissed her neck.

"Petroleum engineering," he said at last, breaking her trance.

"Excuse me?"

"Petroleum engineering. I have a master's degree in petroleum engineering. For undergrad I double-majored in petroleum engineering and geophysics."

She was thunderstruck. "That's not...that's not what I expected. How did you get into that?"

"Long story."

"I've got time."

He blinked slowly at her. The words slurred a little. "One summer when I was seventeen, I worked as a loader at an oil refinery in Bakersfield."

"What's a loader?"

"Just what it sounds like. Loaded up trucks, rail cars. Manual labor." He cleared his throat. "Every day at nine, the engineers rolled into the parking lot, brand-new trucks. Pressed khakis. No cow shit on their shoes. I thought to myself, 'That's it. That's who I want to be.'" Daniel's buzz was wearing off, but his face was still bleary and flushed. He groaned and rubbed his face. "Ugh. Fuck me."

"Take off your boots and lie down," said Georgia. "Have a rest. When you feel sober enough, I'll drive you home."

He did as she told him. He stretched out on the bed and rested his forearm across his eyes, his breaths jagged and uneven.

"Are you going to puke? Because if you are I gotta take precautions," she said, eying the trashcan on the other side of the room.

"Naw, I won't puke," he said. "But this headache is killin' me."

"What helps?"

"Sleep."

"Then do that," she said.

Daniel lifted his arm and looked at her. "It's late. What about you?"

Georgia reached into her bag and pulled out a paperback. "I'll read." She always traveled with books—they made inevitable travel delays almost bearable. "You rest."

"I don't feel right, taking your bed while you sit there." He stared at her for a moment. "Lie down next to me."

She smiled. "I know that trick."

"Don't flatter yourself," he said. "I told you I don't sleep with feminists." Slowly, he got out of bed and pulled off the bedspread. He grabbed the four flat-as-a-pancake pillows and lined them up straight down the middle of the bed. "There. Your side. My side. Fort Knox. Now we're both safe." He lay back down with a grunt. The mattress dipped below his weight.

Georgia stared at him in silence. He rolled onto his side and folded his arm under his head like a makeshift pillow. Soon his breathing evened out. His limbs went slack, and he began to snore softly, the whiskey dragging him under at last.

Ignored, Georgia's book slipped out of her hands as she watched him. Daniel MacKinnon was unlike any character she'd ever seen, in print or in real life. In her eight years as a journalist, Georgia had become convinced that there were sixteen different types of people in the world. If you took the time to listen and observe, every person you met fit into those categories like puzzle pieces.

But Daniel MacKinnon was an outlier. He disproved her theory. From what she'd seen in the morning, he was good at sizing up a situation, weighing his options, and following through. But from what she'd seen at the Silver Spur, he was hotheaded and unpredictable. He was right at home on the ranch, working with his hands, but he also had an advanced degree in engineering, which probably meant his brain was as hard and lean and quick as his body.

Worst of all, he ran hot and cold for her. He insulted her as he flirted with her. He teased her as he seared with those incredible eyes. He was a gentleman and a jerk at the same time.

Georgia was transfixed.

A while ago, she'd convinced herself that men only ever got interesting past the age of thirty-five. Daniel fell short of that mark by eleven years, and he was interesting as hell.

Guess I was wrong.

Quietly, she pulled off her boots and rubbed her arms. The heater in the corner of the motel room was broken. She touched her leather jacket—the leather and satin lining had gone cold. She shuddered, not wanting to put it on.

Deep asleep, Daniel shifted his weight. His heavy arm slid down over Fort Knox, toppling one of the pillows.

He's out cold. Nothing will happen.

Georgia brought her book to the bed, lay down on her side, and pulled the covers up over both of them. Daniel snuggled against the pillows in his sleep, making her heart do goofy little shimmies in her chest. Up close, he smelled like beer—no escaping that—but besides that, he smelled soapy and clean. Georgia took a deep breath. Another scent teased her deep memory.

What was it?

Minutes passed until she finally figured it out—Niagara spray starch. She hadn't smelled that scent in years. Her father used to iron his shirts and slacks with it. The fresh smell reminded her of church on Sunday mornings, but on Daniel, it was sexy. It screamed "grownup."

Georgia settled down, trying to quell the jittery, jumpy energy running up and down her arms and legs. Despite the cool way she tried to act around Daniel, the truth was, she hadn't had a man in her bed for almost five months. Her precarious work situation had left her too busy and stressed to date, much less be in a relationship. In the past, a one-night stand was usually enough to get the edge off. These days, she preferred to take care of the restlessness all by herself. No muss, no fuss.

She opened her book again. The words swam on the page. Nothing stuck. She couldn't remember who the characters were.

Concentrate.

She read the words methodically, getting the meaning of individual sentences but not the gist of the story. For a second time, the book slipped from her hands, landing softly on her chest. Finally, fatigue set in. Georgia drifted off.

ALSO BY MIA HOPKINS

The Cowboy Cocktail Series
Cowboy Valentine
Cowboy Resurrection
Cowboy Player
Cowboy Karma
Cowboy Rising

The Kings of California Series
Deep Down
Hollywood Honkytonk

ABOUT THE AUTHOR

Mia Hopkins writes lush romances starring fun, sexy characters who love to get down and dirty. She's a sucker for working class heroes, brainy heroines and wisecracking best friends. She lives in Los Angeles with her roguish husband and waggish dog.

For more information, please visit her website at **www.miahopkinsauthor.com.**

Made in the USA
Monee, IL
08 December 2020

51681880R00089